THE
CHOSEN
FEW

Cast of Characters

Max Lovely, PI: Protagonist
Mrs. Grybowski: Max's elderly neighbor
Ms. Jaimee Kantor: Max's new client
David Kantor: Estranged husband of Jaimee
The tall, thin man: A prowler
Roland Moore: Architect, David Kantor's business partner
Osmond "Oz" Quinn: Mason, denizen of Boston's South End
Eliot Winthrop Tufton IV: Max's assistant
Allen Pierce: David Kantor's law partner
J. Andrew Winthrop: Classmate of David Kantor from Harvard Law
Marcia Paige: David Kantor's secretary
Judy Winter: Woman seeking to hire a private investigator
Anthony "the Ant" Diaz: Bodyguard, friend of Max
Ralph Henman: Neighbor and owner of the cat, Cyrus
Lou Brenna: "Made" member of the Vermino crime family
Allessandro Vermino: Current don of the Boston mafia
Aaron and Jeffrey Zimmer: Vermino's attorneys
Mayor John Riordan: Mayor of Boston
Charlotte Shearson: Neighbor of David Kantor
Adrienne Forest: David Kantor's rental broker
Marshall Forest: Adrienne's husband
Francine Cheyette: Electronics expert, friend of Max
Lt. Nathan Thomas: Lieutenant, Boston police

CHAPTER ONE

Max Lovely stopped his old Chrysler at the end of his driveway. He could see his neighbor on her front porch, struggling with a plastic trash can in the fading light. He turned off the engine.

"I'll get that for you, Mrs. Grybowski."

She sighed. "This garbage can keeps getting bigger."

"They have a way of doing that." He carried it down to the sidewalk and left it beneath the old maple tree in front of her house.

"You're a very kind young man," she said.

"Well, you're half right." He hadn't even been young a decade ago when she started calling him that.

She laughed. "How about some coffee?"

"Thanks, but I'm on my way to a client."

"A client?! In that shirt?"

Lovely glanced down. "There's a problem? Someone my age would notice?"

"Come on," she said, shaking her head. "A minute with my iron."

Lovely waited shirtless on her couch, chastened, slightly embarrassed, grateful as always for her concern.

"There. Now you'll make a good impression on him," she declared.

"Her."

She raised her eyebrows. "Single?"

"Probably deranged like most of my clients. Thank you, Mrs. Grybowski. Any trash cans give you trouble, call me. You're under my protection."

2

* * * * *

It was past ten p.m. when Lovely turned back onto his street. He lived in Watertown, on the outskirts of Boston, in a neighborhood of boxy two-family houses dating from the early twentieth century. His car rolled past dark windows and deserted sidewalks. As far as he could tell, he was the only person on the block who stayed up past eleven and slept past six.

Lovely's new client, Jaimee Kantor, hadn't seemed unstable. He wasn't so sure about her ex-husband. The man had vanished three weeks earlier only to reappear, wraith-like, at the window of her fifth-floor apartment the previous evening. The unsettling image still preoccupied Lovely, and he was pulling into his driveway before he noticed the alien object on his front porch. He stopped short and squinted at it. A man stood crouched beneath his living room windows. The man sprang to his feet, cleared the porch steps in a stride, and took off down the street.

Lovely spun his car around and stomped on the gas. Out in the open, he could see the man was tall and thin, with broad, angular shoulders. He was wearing coveralls and black leather gloves. He darted onto a side street. Lovely skidded around the corner in time to see him cut in between two houses. Lovely screeched to a stop, jumped out. No one in sight. He raced to the back of the houses, glanced left and right. The maze of connected back yards lay in deep shadow. Lovely ran back to his car for a flashlight and tried again. The light swept over a familiar landscape of detached garages shaded by oaks and maples, a few listing storage sheds, smaller ornamental trees and shrubs, vine-covered trellises. Too much cover. He searched the area for fifteen minutes but turned up nothing. The man could be half a mile away by now.

Lovely went back to his car and drove home. As he passed Mrs. Grybowski's house, he noticed her front door was open. He pulled over. No sign of her on the porch. He

3

climbed the steps and rang the bell. "Mrs. Grybowski?" He rang again. Had she gone out and left the door open? It wouldn't be the first time. He closed it gently and walked back to his car.

Lovely parked in the stand-alone garage at the rear of his house, a frame two-family with faded blue paint. He lived on the first floor beneath his landlord. Lovely took a quick look inside. Nothing appeared out of order. He always secured his doors and windows—a habit gained from years of experience with crime—and had even installed pick-proof locks. He brought his flashlight out to the porch where he had spotted the prowler.

A screen on one of the living room windows was pushed up. He found tool marks, perhaps made by a screwdriver, on the aluminum base of the screen, and hand marks on the dusty sash where the prowler had tried to push open the locked window. Lovely took a closer look at the sash. No fingerprints, just the blank smudges left by the prowler's gloves. The signature of a professional.

Lovely left the porch and started along the base of the house. The east side, adjacent to the driveway, had no cover, and the windows were in plain view of the house next door. None of the screens had been forced. Lovely reached the rear of the building and turned the corner. Two large maples shaded the backyard, their boughs swaying restlessly in the breeze. The house behind was two hundred feet away. Its rear porch light, barely visible, twinkled through the shifting leaves. Lovely shined his flashlight on the first of the windows on the back of his house. It bore tool marks like those on the front.

Something brushed against his leg. He froze. The creature meowed and Lovely let out his breath. It was Cyrus, the giant Persian that lived down the street. Lovely ran his hand over the cat's back and tail. Its fur was as soft as a kitten's, but its jaws were as big as a leopard's. Certain death to any unwary smaller creature. Lovely moved on to the next window. Every screen on the back of the house had been pried open, then closed.

4

The prowler had been very thorough. It would have been easy for him to break a pane of glass and reach through to unlock a window, but he hadn't. Obviously, he put a high premium on his entry going undetected. The apartment contained nothing of monetary value, and a quick look through the windows would have made that apparent, so the attempted break-in probably related to a case. Had Lovely met the burglar before? His shape—tall and thin, with broad, angular shoulders—did not seem familiar.

Lovely moved into the other side yard, dimly illuminated by the lights from Mrs. Grybowski's house. He glanced toward the street. Silent and still. He could hear the hum of the air conditioner in the upstairs apartment. A row of yew trees grew close to this side of the building, providing cover for the prowler to work on the windows. Lovely squeezed between a pair of yews, feeling the dew soak through his shirt. He shined his light on the first window. The screen had been forced. He backed out and moved on to the next window. As he pushed through the yews, his foot came down on something soft. He jerked it back and pointed the flashlight at the ground. An ice-cold feeling gripped his insides. A body. He moved the flashlight to the face. Mrs. Grybowski. He dropped to his knees and grabbed her wrist, searching for a pulse. She was dead.

CHAPTER TWO

The cause of death was strangulation. Lovely could hear the crime scene team at work in the yard, and it might be days before the medical examiner released his report, but he had no doubts: bruising and contusions on the throat, pinpoint hemorrhages on the lips and eyelids, and a shred of black leather snagged on the crucifix Mrs. Grybowski wore around her neck. The prowler had been wearing black gloves.

The two homicide detectives had grilled Lovely for an hour, making him repeat his story again and again, watching for inconsistencies, waiting to pounce like a couple of weasels outside a rat hole. But that was just routine. They quickly realized Lovely knew as little as they, and felt genuine shock and sadness at the death of his neighbor.

"What do you suppose she was doing out in the yard in a bathrobe and slippers?" one of the detectives had asked him.

"I have no idea. She was feisty, but not crazy. She wouldn't confront a prowler at ten o'clock at night."

"Unless she knew the guy."

A possibility Lovely had not considered.

The detectives had Lovely walk through Mrs. Grybowski's apartment, checking for anything out of the ordinary. The living room looked as it had earlier that evening. He had spent a minute staring at the small CD player in the wall unit opposite her bed. Something about it bothered him, but he couldn't put his finger on it.

Lovely let his head fall back against his chair. He knew Mrs. Grybowski's children, and even a few of her grandchildren. He could only imagine the suffering this would bring. As he stared at the ceiling, his thoughts turned back to the prowler. Could the man have known Lovely would be out, meeting with Jaimee Kantor? Lovely hadn't mentioned the appointment to anyone. Jaimee could have sent the man, of course, but he considered it unlikely. He let his thoughts drift back over the events of the evening.

Jaimee lived in a brownstone in Boston's South End. The apartment had been renovated recently, as he could see from the crisp paint and modern baseboard heating units. But the building dated from the 1860's, and traces of its Victorian origins remained: a marble mantelpiece, an ornate plaster medallion above the ceiling light fixture, a three-sided bay window overlooking Tremont Street. The weather was warm for early May, and the windows were open, letting in a night breeze. Lovely could hear the occasional swoosh of a passing car.

"My husband, David, showed up at his office two hours late," Jaimee said, "and told his secretary he was going on vacation. He put a few files in his briefcase and left. He didn't say where he was going or when he was coming back. No one has heard from him in three weeks."

She was sitting on the couch dressed in blue jeans with frayed knees and a white cotton tank top. Her eyes were a startling green, framed by long pale lashes. She wore no jewelry or make-up, and had her light brown hair in a ponytail. She seemed faintly sad—something at the corners of her eyes.

He said, "Your husband left town without telling you where he was going?"

"We've been separated for a year and we're getting a divorce. We're still on good terms, but he wouldn't necessarily tell me about his vacation plans."

"And no one has seen him in three weeks?"

"Not exactly. Last night at about this time, I went to the doorway of our daughter's room to check on her. She was sleeping—she's two. I saw David standing on the balcony, looking in at her through the sliding glass door."

Lovely raised his eyebrows. "Spooky."

"And a shock, too. Living on the top floor, you don't expect to see someone looking in your window. I backed out of the room when I saw him, and when I looked a moment later, he had left."

"How'd he get up there?"

"There's a stair from the balcony up to a roof deck. He must have climbed down from the roof."

"Any idea how he got on the roof?"

She shook her head.

An image came to Lovely of a frightened man, running or hiding from something. An external threat? Some internal anguish?

"So what does it mean?" he asked.

"I have no idea. That's why I called you. Irene Freeman at the Women's Crisis Center recommended you."

"Did you tell her about David?"

"No."

"Why not?"

Jaimee considered the question. "I'm not sure."

"Irene knows several women investigators. She usually recommends them first."

Jaimee smiled. It lit up her face but didn't chase the sadness from her eyes. "Irene said, `If your problem's a stalker, Max Lovely has the qualities that make an impression on a man: he's six foot two, weighs two-thirty, and carries a gun.'"

Lovely smiled. "But your problem's not a stalker."

"No..."

There was silence. A group of people with laughing voices passed by down on Tremont Street. Lovely caught the faint scent of cigarette smoke drifting in through the open windows.

He said, "So you think your husband's in trouble, that it might be something illegal, and possibly dangerous."

Jaimee looked startled. Then her eyes drifted up to the ceiling. After a moment, she nodded slowly. "I hadn't really thought it through, but I suppose you're right—that's been turning around in the back of my mind."

"Does David have a history of breaking the law?"

"Not that I know of."

"Then why do you think he's up to something illegal?"

She paused. "I guess I always had the feeling there were things he wasn't telling me."

"What kind of things?"

"I don't know. It's just a vague feeling."

"What's he do for a living?"

"He's a real estate lawyer. He develops real estate on his own, too, with an architect partner."

"Does he have any mob clients, or is he involved with any loan sharks?"

"Not that I know of."

"Then why do you believe he's into something dangerous?"

A few strands of Jaimee's hair had come loose from her ponytail. She fiddled with them for a minute then pushed them over her shoulder. "I think I've always had the nagging fear he was headed for destruction—like someone who drives too fast and doesn't keep his eyes on the road." She was silent for a minute then shook her head. "You're probably wondering why I would have married a man like that."

"Why did you?"

"I don't know, I guess I was in love with him and didn't stop to think. Maybe that's why it only lasted two years."

She slipped out of her clogs and rubbed a bare foot slowly across the carpet. One toenail was painted pink.

"David's not stupid," she said. "I mean, he's a talented lawyer and a good businessman. He made *Law Review* at Harvard, as he's fond of telling everyone. But he's so intent on becoming a mogul, he doesn't always watch where he's stepping. And the people he surrounds himself with..." She rolled her eyes.

"Like who?"

"His law partner, Allen Pierce, for instance. Allen has good connections, but he's mean-spirited and grim as the reaper. And David's real estate partner, Roland Moore..." She sighed. "Roland, God." She glanced at Lovely, then away.

"Something I should know about you and Roland Moore?"

"No, it doesn't matter. Another mistake." She poked at

9

her clogs with her toe.

Lovely wasn't convinced it didn't matter, but he decided not to press the question yet.

"What is it you want me to do, exactly?" he asked.

"Find out what's going on. I'm worried about David. He might need help, and I don't know if he'd have the sense to ask for it. He thinks all he has to do is turn on his charm, and everything will be ok."

"Maybe you should let him go. He's not your responsibility anymore."

"Our daughter wouldn't think so."

"All right. Where would he go if he was in trouble? Could he be with his family?"

Jaimee shook her head. "I've spoken to them, and to his friends. Nobody has a clue."

"Does he have a girlfriend?"

"Probably—he wouldn't go long without one. But I don't know who."

"Where does he live?"

"Around the corner on West Canton Street. I went by the apartment the other day—it's where we lived together and I still have keys. The air smelled musty. I'll give you the keys if you want to look around."

"I do. I'll need a photograph of him, too. And I'd like to check out your roof."

While Jaimee went in search of a picture, Lovely wandered over to a collection of framed snapshots on the mantel: A baby, presumably her daughter, sitting in a highchair with a bowl of blueberries and a very stained face. The same girl, a bit older, holding a stuffed frog almost as big as herself. There were half a dozen pictures of her and she was only two. By the time she graduated from high school, the mantel would be sagging under the load. Lovely turned to a collection of eight-by-tens on the wall. They were of dark-skinned men and women in a jungle setting, naked except for body paint. They might have been Polynesians or South American Indians. Jaimee had mentioned she taught anthropology at Northeastern University.

Jaimee returned. "This is the only one I could find," she said, slightly embarrassed.

In the picture, Jaimee and David stood side by side, arms around each other. David had a handsome, friendly face and an athletic physique. There was something restive in his posture, as if he were finished posing for the photograph and ready to move on to the next activity. Jaimee wore a white sun dress and white earrings. Her untethered hair shone in the bright sunlight.

"It was a party," she said, glancing down at her tank top and frayed jeans and suddenly sounding a bit apologetic. "I don't usually dress up."

"I'm not offended. You kept your shoes on for the first half hour I was here."

Jaimee laughed. "Come on, I'll show you the deck." She led him through her bedroom to the balcony. "There's a spiral stair up to the roof. I'll wait for you inside."

CHAPTER THREE

Lovely climbed up to Jaimee's roof and stood on her deck, looking out over the South End. Tremont Street, a broad and busy boulevard, ran through the heart of the neighborhood. Rows of attached Victorian townhouses, some brownstone, some brick, lined the street on both sides. It was past nine and traffic was sparse. Overhead, stars shone dimly through the humid haze. A century ago, the South End had been a neighborhood of tenements and rooming houses, home to successive waves of immigrants from Ireland, Greece, Eastern Europe, China, and the Middle East. Blacks from the American South came in great numbers during the boll weevil infestations of the Teens and Twenties. Latinos arrived in the Fifties and Sixties, and a large gay population established itself in the Seventies, as the South End began its renaissance. It remained Boston's most diverse neighborhood.

Jaimee's apartment stood in a block of identical bow-front buildings. The roofs were flat, with two-foot-high brick parapet walls marking the boundary of each townhouse. Lovely could see a pair of skylights on each roof, a large one at the front and a smaller one at the rear. The only other vertical outlines were chimneys, rising waist-high above the level of the roofs.

He climbed over the deck railing and headed out across the block of buildings. The warm, still air smelled of ailanthus and roof tar. He stepped over a parapet wall.

"Good evening, Mister Lovely."

Lovely jumped. A man was sitting on the front edge of the roof, legs dangling in space. A chimney had blocked Lovely's view of him from the deck.

"Oz?"

12

"Who else would be lounging on a rooftop in the South End?"

"What are you doing up here?"

"I'm on top of the world, looking down on gentrification."

Lovely grinned. He had met Osmond Quinn while working on a case a few years back, and had been running into him in odd places ever since. He didn't mind.

"Have a seat," Oz said, waving him over.

"No thanks. You may be a cat, but I'm a buffalo—and not fond of heights." Lovely sat on the parapet wall, well away from the edge of the roof.

Oz was half a foot shorter than Lovely, with a slender, muscular build. He had a wry smile that matched his tone of voice. Oz's family had been in the South End for several generations, and traces of the diverse neighborhood's populace showed through in his dusky, fine-boned Latino face, his African-American gait and patois, and his pale blue eyes and Irish surname.

"What brings you to Tremont Street?" Lovely asked.

"I rebuilt that chimney a few weeks back and took a liking to this spot."

Oz was a mason. His talent for knowing everyone and everything in the South End, however, surpassed even his great skill with bricks and mortar.

"Well, maybe you can answer a question for me." Lovely gestured over his shoulder. "That's the only unit with a roof deck. Is there another way up here without a fifty-foot ladder?"

"Sure, there's a head house on the end building of each block."

Lovely squinted into the darkness. Fifty yards away, he could make out the silhouette of what looked like a small shed. The end building across the street had a similar structure.

"If you can get through the front door," Oz said, "you can take the stairs up to the roof. That's what I do."

"You have a key?"

"Nah, I spring the lock with a pocket knife."

Lovely chuckled. "You have *chutzpah* Oz, I'll say that for you."

"That's Jewish for balls, right?"

"More or less."

"Then yeah, I got it."

"Just be careful. It's been a while since I left the police force, so I may be out of touch, but we used to call that breaking and entering. We used to arrest people for it."

"I'm sure you did, Officer Lovely, but don't get tense: I know the man who owns the building. He loves my blue-eyed Puerto Rican ass. I do work for him all the time. He owns this one, too."

"Ahh. Wouldn't happen to be a guy named David Kantor, would it?"

"Yeah, it would."

Lovely nodded thoughtfully. Sharing his clients' secrets was not something he did without good cause. But Oz he could trust, and depend upon to be well informed.

"I need your help, Oz. David Kantor's missing. His wife just hired me to track him down."

One corner of Oz's mouth turned up. "Beautiful woman hires you to find her husband—sounds like a conflict of interest, Mister Lovely."

"They split up."

Oz winked. "I know. Tell me what's happening."

Oz listened in silence, staring down at the empty street five stories beneath his swinging feet. When Lovely finished, Oz said, "Huh," and kept staring. The traffic light at the intersection was in its nighttime setting, one side flashing yellow, the other red. A taxi, rattling like it was about to fall apart, hurtled through the red light without slowing down.

"I saw David on the roof that night," Oz said.

"Did he see you?"

"No, I was leaning back against the chimney. I wondered what he was doing, but I figured, what the hell, it's his roof."

"Where did he go when he left?"

"Drove off down Tremont Street in his white BMW."

14

Oz nodded toward the west.

"If you see him again, will you call me?"

"Of course."

"And will you ask around for me—see if he might have been up to anything shady?"

Oz winked an eye at him. "The lovely Miss Jaimee couldn't answer that for you?"

"She had only the vaguest suspicions."

"Those are the most interesting kind. I'll see what I can do."

Now, two hours later, Lovely sat slumped in his swivel chair, listening to the crackle of the police radios outside and wondering if the prowler had known he would be out. If so, he didn't believe Jaimee had given the man the information—at least not intentionally. He hadn't sensed any deceptiveness, and his instincts were rarely in error. Even an expert liar couldn't fool him for long.

Doors slammed out on the street. An engine revved. Lovely went to the living room windows. Cars were pulling away. The lonely anti-climax to every crime-scene investigation, abandoning the spot to its grisly memories. This time, though, the body on the way to the morgue was not a nameless victim; it was Mrs. Grybowski. Lovely couldn't quite believe she was dead—that she would never again bring him leftovers, or scrutinize his female visitors from her front porch.

The last cruiser switched off its flashing lights and headed off down the street. Lovely watched it pass out of sight. A nagging thought had been turning around at the back of his mind. He hadn't seen the prowler's face, but the prowler wouldn't know that. He might assume Lovely could identify him. Lovely wondered if he'd be coming back.

CHAPTER FOUR

David Kantor's office was located downtown in Center Plaza, a long brick-and-concrete building which curved to follow a bend in Cambridge Street. There were several entrances spread out along the block. Lovely found the address he was looking for and rode the elevator to the fourth floor.

He had spent the morning making routine phone calls. Kantor had not applied for electrical, gas, or telephone service recently. The post office was forwarding his mail to his office. National Crime Information Center database had no records on David Kantor, nor was he known to the Boston police. Lovely's last call had been to his own assistant, Eliot Tufton, whom he had dispatched to the registry of deeds to research the properties David owned. Lovely wanted to know who held David's mortgages, and whether there were any attachments—mechanics' liens, tax liens, lis pendens— anything that might shed light on David's financial situation. He had also walked through David's condominium and stopped by Jaimee's office at Northeastern to return her keys.

Lovely opened a heavy oak door and stepped into the offices of Pierce and Kantor, Attorneys at Law. The reception room had three large windows facing Government Center. With a telescope, one could have peered into the office of Mayor Keith Riordan, to watch him bask in his power, popularity, and boyish good looks. Lovely was greeted by a petite, skinny, red-haired woman seated behind an L-shaped desk.

"May I help you?" She had a tiny voice to match her sparrow-like frame. Lovely had the feeling he could put her to flight with one loud cough. He summoned up his friendliest tone. He had been accused, more than once, of coming across as grouchy.

"My name's Max Lovely. I'd like to speak to Mr. Pierce, please."

"Will he know what this is regarding?"

"No."

There was silence for a moment. The woman shifted uncomfortably. "Mr. Pierce is very busy. He may not see you, if he doesn't know what this is regarding."

"Ok, I'm a private investigator working for David Kantor's wife. She's concerned about his absence."

Her eyes widened for a moment. Mechanically, she picked up the phone and relayed the information to Allen Pierce.

"Mr. Pierce will see you now." She directed him to Pierce's office without making eye contact.

Pierce rose to his feet and reached across his desk to shake Lovely's hand. A few inches shorter than Lovely, he had white-blond hair and pale skin. His face, handsome but marred by acne, was impassive.

"Pleased to meet you," he said in a toneless voice. He motioned Lovely to a leather chair. Lovely wondered if people accused Pierce of being grouchy. Maybe they could share about the experience.

Lovely repeated what he had told the secretary. "It's been three weeks and Ms. Kantor is growing concerned. Do you have any idea where David might be?"

"No."

Lovely waited for Pierce to say more. He didn't. You could learn a lot by the way a man answered his first question.

"Did David mention anything in the days before he left that might explain why he went away so suddenly?"

"No."

"Was he working on any particular case that might account for his departure?"

"Not that I'm aware of."

"Can you think of anyone David might be running from? A potentially dangerous client, for example."

"No."

Was Pierce being uncooperative, or was he just taciturn by nature? Maybe a different approach would draw him out.

"I've never met David. What can you tell me about him?"

"The question is too broad."

"Wait, don't tell me...you're a lawyer."

"I beg your pardon?"

"A tall, thin man was prowling around my house last night," Lovely said. "Does David know anyone who fits that description and might do something like that?"

"Not to my knowledge."

"Was he litigating against anyone who might have threatened him?"

"Not that I know of."

Lovely paused. Pierce was obviously not taxing his mind in search of answers.

"Are you concerned about him, Mr. Pierce?"

"Is there any reason to think some harm has befallen him?"

Lovely tapped his pencil on his pad. "How do you and David get along?"

"Fine."

"And if he never comes back?"

"He said he was going on vacation. Is there any reason to think he won't come back?"

Lovely leaned back in his chair. "Do you get pissed off when people answer your questions with questions?"

Pierce's face twitched. "I have work to do, and I've told you all I know. Good luck with your search."

Lovely gave a mental shrug. He wasn't learning anything, or even having fun.

"Thanks. Let's do this again sometime." He stuffed his still-blank note pad in his pocket and left.

As Lovely passed through the reception area, the secretary caught his eye. She gave him an intent, almost pleading look. He took a business card from his pocket and dropped it on her desk as he walked out.

CHAPTER FIVE

Roland Moore's architectural firm was located on Newbury Street, in a neighborhood known as the Back Bay. The area had actually been a bay at one time, a tidal flat at the Charles River estuary. By the mid-nineteenth century, with Boston's population growing rapidly, the bay reeked of sewage at low tide, and the city fathers resolved to fill it in. Broad, French-inspired boulevards were laid out on the filled land, and house lots sold. The new homes were larger and more architecturally distinct than those of the South End, where Jaimee Kantor lived. The South End, with its narrow streets and small English squares, began to seem old-fashioned. Upper-class Bostonians soon abandoned it in favor of the Back Bay, and the South End entered a period of decline that would last a hundred years.

In recent decades, Newbury Street had become the Back Bay's boutique district. Its converted brownstones now housed art galleries, antique shops, and trendy clothing stores. Clusters of white-clothed cafe tables dotted the sidewalk. On the way from Center Plaza, Lovely had changed his assessment of the Pierce interview. He had learned something after all: Allen Pierce was in no hurry for his partner to return. And his secretary was as scared as a rabbit.

Roland Moore's office was situated between a shoe store with an Italian name and a French hairdresser. The reception room had glass walls and a blue glass ceiling that arched upward like a cathedral. Above it, Lovely could see nothing but diffused light, creating the illusion of sky. The walls were decorated with framed photographs of houses—designed by Moore, Lovely presumed—which resembled fish tanks stuck together at odd angles. At the center of the room sat the receptionist, a long-limbed blonde in a white dress. She looked as if Moore had taken her out of a Fifth Avenue window display and brought her to life. Or almost to life: she had a smile as inert as a mannequin's.

"May I help you?" she asked.

"I'm here to see Roland Moore. My name's Max Lovely. He won't know me, but you can tell him I was sent by Jaimee Kantor. I just need to ask him a few questions."

The receptionist continued to smile at Lovely while he spoke, until the corners of her mouth began to quiver from the strain. It was fatiguing to watch.

"One moment," she said. She picked up the phone and spoke to Moore. "He'll see you now," she said to Lovely. "His office is at the end of the hall, last door on the right." She hadn't stopped smiling.

"You don't have to feel obliged to smile at me," Lovely said gently. "I can see you're helpful and polite."

She looked startled, then indignant. An instant later, she realized he wasn't mocking her. The tension drained from her body and her eyes took on a glimmer of life. She didn't say anything, but Lovely thought he felt a silent "thank you" as he went past her desk.

Lovely found Roland Moore carefully arrayed on a sofa in his office. He was over six feet tall, broad-shouldered, with lots of dark hair and very photogenic cheek bones. He wore a charcoal-gray sport jacket made of fine Italian wool and a crisp, perfectly tailored white cotton shirt. Lovely wondered if he should apologize for not having brought his camera.

Moore rose to his feet and shook Lovely's hand. "Please, have a seat." He gestured to an armchair. The office contained a desk and a computer, too, but they appeared to be afterthoughts.

"I spoke to Jaimee this morning on another matter," Moore said in a friendly tone. "She mentioned your comment about her keeping her shoes on for the first half hour." He leaned back on the couch, an amused smile on his face.

Lovely eyed him, trying to determine what was out of place. Beneath the smile, Moore seemed ill at ease.

"When you spoke to her on the `other matter,' did she mention she's very worried about David?"

Moore adjusted his expression, belatedly, to reflect concern. "Yes, of course. We're all a little uneasy about his absence."

"Any idea where he might have gone?"

"None."

"Why do you suppose he left on such short notice?"

Moore shook his head. "I really don't know. It's not like him to do this kind of thing."

"Was he having financial problems?"

"Not that I know of. Our projects are doing fine."

"Any problems with the union?"

"Never."

Lovely didn't have the impression Moore was lying, but he seemed overeager to profess his ignorance.

"How come you're nervous, Mr. Moore?"

Moore cocked his head. "Nervous? I'm not nervous."

Now Lovely had the impression he was lying.

"Can you think of anyone who might have a grudge against David?"

"No, he's not the type to make enemies."

"How do you get along with him?"

"Very well."

"How's he feel about you sleeping with his wife?"

Moore's smile crumpled like a paper flower under a boot. "They split up a year ago, and he doesn't know about it. Not that it's any of your business."

"So why is this interview making you tense?"

Moore's face tightened. Lovely gave another mental shrug. Some days, he pissed off everyone.

"I told you," Moore said, "it's not."

Still lying. Lovely could feel one of the dependable alerts he experienced in the presence of duplicity—a kind of empathetic embarrassment, like watching a bad actor in a play.

"Was David doing business with anyone dangerous?" Lovely asked. "A loan shark, for example."

"Not that I know of."

21

"A tall, thin guy, probably a killer, was prowling around my house last night. Know anything about that?"

Moore's eyes widened. "No!"

That, at least, seemed like an honest response.

"If David was running from someone," Lovely said, "they'd be looking for him. Has anyone else asked about him?"

Something flickered across Moore's face. A direct hit.

"Who?" Lovely asked.

"No one in particular," Moore said quickly. "Naturally, a number of our business associates have wondered about David's surprise vacation. But no strangers have come looking for him."

Lovely eyed him. The response was almost believable, but it didn't explain the flicker. "Any other private investigators?"

"No."

"Police?"

"No, I told you, no one but our regular business associates."

Lovely nodded slowly. "I hate listening to BS, don't you?"

Moore's mouth opened then closed. He took a calming breath. "Look, I'm trying to be helpful, and I don't appreciate the implication."

"Ok. Let's make a list of everyone who asked about David. That would be really helpful. Names and occupations."

Moore reeled off a dozen names—contractors, real estate brokers, insurance agents. Lovely didn't expect the name he was looking for to make the list, but at least his note pad had something on it.

Lovely thanked Moore for his time and departed. On the way out, he waved to the receptionist. She smiled at him, then caught herself and stopped, then smiled again, then burst out laughing.

CHAPTER SIX

Lovely reclined in his swivel chair, eyes closed, feet on his desk. His mind worked best when his body was in repose. He let his thoughts drift. They floated in circles for a minute then bumped into a fact: Roland Moore was a liar. Someone else was looking for David. But why would Moore want to hide that? Lovely's mind floated for another minute then bumped. Moore had something to hide, too. Certainly, having his partner out of the way would make it easier for him to pursue his "other matters" with Jaimee.

Then there was Allen Pierce. The man had a personality that could freeze Prestone II and a poker face even Lovely couldn't read. Maybe David was running from Pierce.

Then there was the prowler—too thin to be Moore and too tall to be Pierce. Three bad guys and no good guys. Lovely shook his head. The odds were turning against him already.

The phone rang. With a grunt, he sat up and yanked it off the hook.

"Lovely, here," he growled.

"What's the matter with your cranky ass, Mister Lovely?"

Lovely snorted. "Sorry, Oz. Did I hurt your feelings?"

"That's better. I asked around about David Kantor. He's no Mother Theresa, Mister Lovely."

Lovely sighed and leaned back in his chair. *Four* bad guys and no good guys. "Go on."

"The building inspectors love to shake his hand, because his hand is never empty. The board of appeals gives him everything he asks for, and he gives the board members everything they ask for. The city councilmen open their doors for him, because they know his wallet will open for them. That's your boy, Mister Lovely."

"What about Roland Moore?"

"There are no secrets between the two."

"That's what you think."

"Huh?"

"Does David burn buildings," Lovely asked, "or steal money, or run around with loan sharks?"

"No."

"Then why the hell did he drop out of sight?"

"No one seems to know."

Lovely sighed. "Got any *good* news for me, Oz?"

"The stock market closed down."

"Glad to hear it."

Lovely put down the phone and closed his eyes. Maybe tomorrow he'd meet some good guys.

The doorbell rang.

"Go away," Lovely growled.

It rang again.

"This better be good."

Lovely opened the door, and his assistant, Eliot Tufton, burst into the room, waving a sheaf of papers over his head.

"Boy, do I have a story for you! Kantor doesn't borrow from a bank, he borrows from a private lender—and the guy's a Winthrop! But a fake Winthrop, according to my dad. And that's not all: the clerk at the registry of deeds..." Eliot's voice trailed off. He glanced around the room. "Cripes, Max, this place is starting to look bad. It's even worse than mine."

"Yeah, but I've spent years getting it this way. You have your apartment cleaned every week, and two days later, it looks like the L.L. Bean store after a tidal wave."

"That's true." Eliot pushed aside a pile of newspapers and sat down on the couch. He was wearing a light blue Oxford shirt, khakis, and Topsiders. He was twenty-eight years old, six feet tall, and he still couldn't buy liquor without two forms of ID. They had met a few years back when Eliot hired Lovely to recover some stolen artwork. When the case was over, Lovely offered him a job. Thanks to his trust fund,

Eliot didn't need employment, and in truth, Lovely didn't need an assistant. They had worked together on every case since.

Lovely sat down across from him. He wasn't feeling cranky anymore. "So, what were you yelling about?"

"Oh, the clerk. I asked him a question about one of David's properties, and he said, `David Kantor... Were you the guy I spoke to yesterday?' I said, `No, was someone else looking up Kantor's property?' He said, `Yes.'

"Well, I tried to get a name or a description, but the clerk had no memory of the guy at all—he talks to hundreds of people every day. All he remembered was the name, David Kantor, because his uncle's name is David and he's a cantor. By the way, Max, when he said, 'cantor', he made it sound like a job or something?"

"A cantor is the person who leads the singing in a synagogue."

"Oh." Eliot paused. "I don't think I'd like that job."

"No, you're not cut out for it. Now what's this about a private lender?"

"Right. Most of Kantor's loans are from a guy named J. Andrew Winthrop."

"Winthrop's your middle name, right?"

"Right. My great-great-grandfather married a Winthrop. His son was Eliot Winthrop Tufton the First."

"And you're the Fourth."

"Exactly. So I called my dad to ask if this guy J. Andrew was related to us. He got all irate and said those Winthrops didn't even come to this country until the end of the seventeenth century; they're not even related to John Winthrop, never mind being descended from him, but they go around naming their kids John because they think they can fool people that way, and they're all a pack of social climbers and liars, and besides, they made their money in the triangular trade."

"How the hell does your father know all that?"

"Are you kidding? He knows every Winthrop in the country. He has our family tree memorized back to the Stone

Age."

Lovely shook his head. "John Winthrop was a Pilgrim, wasn't he?"

"A Pilgrim?! Come on, Max. John Winthrop was the first governor of the Massachusetts Bay Colony. He founded Boston. The Pilgrims were down in Plymouth. Didn't they teach you American History at Dorchester High?"

"I was looking out the window that semester. So these fake Winthrops—they're in the mortgage business?"

"That's just it: they're not. My dad says they own a lot of commercial real estate, but they don't lend money. And as a banker, he'd know."

One of Eliot's ancestors had founded Boston Bank and Trust two centuries earlier, and the family still owned it.

"So there's something special going on between J. Andrew Winthrop and David Kantor," Lovely said.

"Looks that way."

Lovely nodded. He checked the list of names Moore had recited. Winthrop was not on it.

"Refresh my memory," Lovely said. "What was the triangular trade?"

"Max! I can't believe..."

Lovely raised his hand. "Just answer the question. You didn't know what a cantor was."

"All right. New England traders would bring molasses up from the West Indies and make it into rum. Then they'd take the rum to Africa and trade it for slaves. Then they'd carry the slaves to the West Indies and trade them for molasses."

"Right. Now I remember why I forgot." Lovely shook his head. "The Puritans were involved in that?"

"Absolutely."

"Makes you wonder what god they were worshipping."

"What god?"

"Money," Lovely said.

"Oh. They worshipped money all right; and not just money, but success. They saw it as a mark of divine favor."

"Chosen by God to get rich in immoral ways."

26

"Yeah, it is kind of twisted."

"Do you have an address for this descendant of slave-traders?"

"Sure, it's on every mortgage." Eliot handed him the sheaf of documents. Winthrop lived at Louisburg Square, on Beacon Hill.

"Did you find any evidence that Kantor's having financial problems?" Lovely asked.

"No, but that doesn't prove anything. These loans could be in default and I wouldn't know unless notices of foreclosure had been filed."

Lovely nodded. "There's a file cabinet in Kantor's condo packed with business files. I'd like you to go through it. You know more about this stuff than I do, with your MBA and your years at the bank."

"Ok."

"I'll call Jaimee and tell her you'll stop by in the morning to pick up keys. She doesn't leave her apartment until ten."

When Eliot was gone, Lovely returned to his room and took up the position he had relinquished to answer the door. A pair of thirty-gallon fish tanks stood along the wall adjacent to his desk. The one on the right—the new one—housed a freshwater gar, six inches long. It hovered motionless on the far end of the tank, staring at the fish in the other aquarium. Lovely grimaced. Time to feed the creature.

Lovely scooped a net-full of guppies from a goldfish bowl and dropped them into the gar's tank. The gar drifted toward them. It was brown in color and as thin as Lovely's little finger. It looked like a floating stick—which was the objective. The gar brought its snout up next to a large female, then snapped its head sideways and caught the little fish in its beak. The guppy wriggled frantically. The gar moved its jaws a few times, adjusting its grip, then swallowed the guppy whole.

Lovely turned away. He had tried feeding the gar flake food, pellet food, frozen food. But if a creature wasn't alive, the gar didn't recognize it as edible. So Lovely fed it guppies and watched it grow—two inches in the month he'd had it.

Lovely turned to look at his other aquarium. These fish didn't eat each other. He adjusted his feet on the desk to give them a more comfortable lie. He listened to the bubbling of the under-gravel filter and felt the rise and fall of his chest. "Noticing," he called it. He spent hours at it, whenever he could. That mind worked best, which worked least.

An hour later, the phone rang. Lovely leaned forward and picked it up.

"My name is Marcia Paige," the caller said in a low, urgent voice. "I'm the secretary at Pierce and Kantor. I need to speak to you as soon as possible."

Lovely could hear traffic sounds in the background. "Where are you?"

"Cambridge Street. I just got off work."

"You have a car?"

"Yes."

"Come over now." Lovely gave her directions and hung up. He stared at the phone for a minute, wondering what she was so anxious to tell him. Then he leaned back in his chair, closed his eyes, and picked up his "noticing" where he had left off.

CHAPTER SEVEN

Lovely apologized for the mess and seated Marcia Paige in the space Eliot had cleared on the couch. She put her hands in her lap and pressed her spindly arms against her sides.

"Would you like something to drink?" Lovely asked. "I probably have coffee or tea or something. I know I have water."

She shook her head.

"That makes it easier. All my cups are in the sink."

She smiled a little. Lovely congratulated himself on his polished social graces.

"So, you wanted to speak to me?"

She nodded.

"I'm ready to listen."

"It's...about David."

"Yes."

"On the day he left," she said carefully, "he came by the office. He told me he needed a break and was going on vacation. He hadn't decided where he was going yet or when he was coming back—'maybe a few weeks,' he told me. It was all so sudden and strange. I think that's why I went to the window after he walked out."

Lovely nodded encouragingly. "What did you see?"

"I saw him cross the street to his car, a BMW Roadster. I noticed his driver's-side window was broken—there was nothing left but a few pieces around the edge. And below it, on the door, I saw some kind of round black spot. I didn't think much of it at the time—just a break-in, I assumed, and the door got scratched. But now I wonder..." Her voice trailed off. She glanced anxiously at Lovely.

"Could it have been a bullet hole?" he asked.

"It kind of looked like one."

Lovely tapped his foot.

"Did David seem anxious that day, or upset?"

"No, but that doesn't mean anything. He always makes you think everything's ok." Her words were flowing more easily, now. "There could be a hundred clients waiting in his office—angry, panicked, in tears. David could walk in and close the door, and ten minutes later, they'd all come out smiling. He can make anyone happy."

"Or almost anyone," Lovely suggested. "Any idea who'd shoot at him?"

Marcia's eyes narrowed and she leaned forward in her seat. "Allen Pierce!" she spat, with such venom it made Lovely jump.

"Why?"

"Because David has the clients. When the phone rings, it's for David, when the mail comes, it's for David, when someone walks through the door, it's for David." Her voice was rising. "But *now*, suddenly, Allen has all the clients he could ever want. He has David's files, so David's clients are falling into his lap."

As a police detective, Lovely had investigated plenty of murders motivated by greed. But this...

"You really believe Allen would kill David for his clients?"

"Oh, it's not just that: Allen *hates* David. He's jealous because everyone likes David and no one likes him."

"Still, it's one thing to hate someone and another to shoot at him."

"Allen could do it. He's the meanest, most vicious person I've ever met. His poor ex-wife. He used to grab her by the throat and shake her when he got angry—she told me about it."

Lovely grimaced at the image. Still, it didn't make Pierce a murderer, and experience had taught him to be skeptical of an ex-spouse's testimony.

"How does David feel about Allen?" Lovely asked.

"He can't stand him."

"Why did he go into business with him?"

"Because Allen's father is William Pierce."

"Who's that?"

Her eyes widened. "He's the managing partner of Bradford and Pierce!"

"That's a law firm, right?"

"Yes! The most prestigious in the city. David and Allen worked there together for five years before they went off on their own."

"Five years in the same firm and David didn't figure out what kind of guy Allen was?"

She shook her head. "When David wants something badly enough, he has this way of blinding himself. Allen seemed like the perfect choice for a partner because his last name is so well known."

"Why did Allen go into business with David?"

Her eyes took on the nasty squint again. "I think he just wanted to screw over his father—to leave B and P and take the firm's best associate with him."

"If he's so bad, why do you stay?"

"Because of David—I was his secretary at B and P. And now he's been gone for *weeks*, and I'm stuck there with that *creep*..." Her eyes filled up with tears.

"It must be awful."

"It *is* awful! He's the meanest, most horrible person I've ever met. He's always coming up with little snide comments to hurt your feelings. When you make a mistake, he rubs your face in it. He hates himself and takes it out on everyone else, and he hates me because I like David, and now David's gone..." She burst into tears.

Lovely handed her a box of Kleenex.

"He's been gone for weeks," she sobbed, "and he doesn't even call in for his messages, and I don't know if he's dead or alive!"

"He's alive."

"How do you know?" she demanded contemptuously.

"Because Jaimee saw him through her window the other

night."

Marcia looked up, mascara running down her cheeks. "That *bitch*! She knows I'm worried sick about him and she doesn't even call me! She's as bad as Allen, the little JAP—she doesn't care about anyone but herself!"

When Marcia stopped crying, she took a mirror from her purse and wiped the mascara off her face with a Kleenex.

"Please don't tell Allen I spoke to you," she said. "I don't know what he might do."

"Of course not."

She gave a little nod of acknowledgement, then folded her Kleenex and tried to look composed.

"How about that drink of water I offered you?" Lovely asked.

"Please, if you have a clean glass."

He brought it to her in a paper cup.

She took a sip. "I'm afraid my behavior wasn't very professional."

Lovely shrugged. "Why would you want to behave like a professional? Better to be human."

While Marcia demurely sipped her water, Lovely pondered her hypothesis that Pierce had made an attempt on David's life. It was plausible, perhaps, but why wouldn't David have reported it to the police? Did Pierce have someone to back him up?

"Has Pierce had any dealings with mobsters?" Lovely asked.

"Not that I know of."

"Does he have anything going with Roland Moore?"

"I don't think so. But he's so secretive, anything's possible. He has a whole cabinet full of files he won't let anyone touch."

Lovely nodded thoughtfully. "I better have a look at them."

"He'd never let you."

"I realize that. Do you have a key to the office?"

Marcia's eyes widened. "You're not going to...sneak in there?!"

"If you give me the key, I will."

"I couldn't! Mr. Lovely, *please*."

"Not even for David?"

She heaved a sigh. "I don't know... It wouldn't help you anyway, because I don't have the key to Allen's private office."

"That's ok. Once I'm in the reception area, I can take my time with Allen's door."

"Take your... What do you mean?!"

"Maybe you shouldn't ask."

"Oh!" She took another sip of water.

"Does Allen work late?"

"He has been, recently. He was still there when I left. If you must go in, why don't you wait till the middle of the night?"

"That might make the building security guards suspicious. Any chance Allen will come back once he leaves for the evening?"

"I don't think so. Maybe if he left something important behind, but it's a half-hour drive in from Lincoln."

"Ok, then I'd like the key, please."

"I can't believe I'm doing this," she muttered, and thrust her hand into her purse.

Lovely grinned. "Isn't it nice not having to behave like a professional?"

* * * * *

As soon as Marcia left, Lovely called Eliot.

"I just spoke to someone who thinks she saw a bullet hole in David's car door."

Lovely could hear Eliot suck in his breath.

"Yeah. Better take the Ant when you go into David's apartment tomorrow." Eliot wasn't a licensed PI, yet, and didn't have a permit to carry a gun. Anthony "the Ant" Diaz had a permit—and an attitude to go with it.

"Ok." Eliot's tone suggested his true preference would be to skip the visit altogether.

"Attaboy. You can brief the Ant on the case, but don't mention the bullet hole to Jaimee—not till I'm more certain that's what it was."

"All right."

Lovely hung up and called Jaimee. The phone rang several times. He found himself wondering if Roland Moore were visiting her on "another matter." She picked up.

"Am I disturbing you?" Lovely asked.

"No, I was just getting out of the shower. Have you found out what's going on?"

"No, I called because I have some questions."

"Go ahead."

"Apparently, David has borrowed a lot of money from a private lender named J. Andrew Winthrop. Know anything about that?"

"Sure. Andrew was a classmate of David's at Harvard Law. He has family money."

"Are he and David friends?"

She laughed. "Well, David's friends with everyone, you know. But with Andrew, I think it's mostly a business relationship. The only times I met him were at Harvard functions."

"Is Andrew in the business of money-lending?"

She paused. "I'm not sure. I never had the sense he was a professional banker or anything."

"What does he do?"

"He's a lawyer. I know he handles his family's legal work—they own real estate. I don't know if he has outside clients as well. He certainly wouldn't need them."

"Ok. I'm going to pay him a visit tomorrow, see what he knows. Also, I want my assistant, Eliot Tufton, to look through a file cabinet in David's condo. Can I send him by your apartment in the morning for keys?"

"No problem."

Lovely heard a plaintive meowing and glanced up. The big Persian was on the outside sill looking dolefully through the window. Lovely sighed. "Hang on a second. This cat won't shut up till I let him in." He opened the window and the cat jumped through and hopped up on the bed.

"Got a soft spot for cats?" Jaimee asked.

"I guess so. One more question: Someone tried to break into my apartment while I was meeting you last night— a tall, thin guy with broad, angular shoulders. Know anyone like that?"

"Doesn't sound familiar."

"Did you tell anybody about our appointment?"

"I don't think so." She paused. "No, not anyone."

CHAPTER EIGHT

It was 8:10 p.m. when Lovely parked across the street from Center Plaza. Most of the windows were dark, but those on the fourth floor above Entrance Three were still lit. Allen Pierce was making money. Lovely took two pairs of latex gloves from his pocket and tossed one to Oz.

"Always feel sleazy doing stuff like this," Lovely muttered.

Oz grinned. "It's been a while since I left the police force," he said, repeating Lovely's words from the night before in an imitation of Lovely's gruff voice, "so I may be out of touch. But we used to call this breaking and entering."

"How'd you get so funny, Oz?"

At 8:35 p.m., the lights in Pierce's office blinked out. A minute later, Pierce came out of the building. He crossed Cambridge Street and headed toward the Government Center garage, where Marcia said he customarily parked.

"Let's give him fifteen minutes to make sure he doesn't change his mind," Lovely said.

At eight-fifty, they climbed out of the car and crossed the empty street. A warm breeze was blowing from behind them, carrying the muted sounds of street musicians at Quincy Market, a block away. The lobby of Three Center Plaza was deserted. Lovely unlocked the lobby door with Marcia's key and they went in. They were dressed in jackets and ties, but he doubted they looked like attorneys. They rode the elevator to the fourth floor. The dimly-lit hall was empty. Lovely glanced at the space beneath the door to the offices of Pierce and Kantor. The lights were off inside. Marcia's key opened the lock and they stepped in. They donned their latex gloves and Lovely locked the door behind them. He switched on the lights.

Oz raised his eyebrows. "You're the burglary expert, Mister Lovely, but don't you think we'd be better off with a flashlight?"

"If a cop goes by outside and sees a flashlight beam bouncing around, he'll guess it's not lawyers making finger shadows."

Oz shook his head. "Guess I just feel safer in the dark."

"Come on, let's get this done quick."

Oz knelt down in front of Pierce's office door. "It's a Schlage. This won't be easy."

He took out a collection of picks and tension wrenches and selected one of each. They looked like pieces of heavy wire with oddly-shaped tips. He inserted the tension wrench into the keyhole and held it in place with his left hand. With his right, he slipped in the pick and went to work, moving the pins into position. Lovely stood by, eyes shifting between Oz and the front door. He wiped his palms on his pant legs.

"Is it going to work?"

"Don't know yet."

Oz let go of the pick, flexed his hand a few times, and tried again. "Come on, *tesoro*." He turned the tension wrench, and the door swung open.

"Check the desk," Lovely said. "I'll get the file cabinet."

Oz went around behind the desk. "It's locked."

"So's the goddam cabinet."

Oz started on the file cabinet. Lovely sat down on the desk, stood back up, looked through the neatly-stacked piles of papers on Pierce's conference table. They were corporate ledgers pertaining to a breach of contract suit. He sat down again and tapped his foot.

"Got it!" Oz said. He moved to the desk.

Lovely yanked open the top drawer and pulled out the first file. *Pierce vs. Pierce.* He had worked on enough divorce cases to be familiar with the paperwork. Nothing appeared out of order. It was reasonable that Pierce would keep his own divorce files private. Lovely hurried out to the photocopier in the reception area and made a copy of Pierce's personal financial statement, just in case.

"Open sesame," Oz said, and pulled out the center drawer of Pierce's desk. "Tape, stapler, bottle of White Out. Wonder if that would work on you, Mister Lovely."

"Quiet," Lovely growled. He shoved the divorce papers back in the cabinet and grabbed the next file. *Jasper vs. Swoboda Construction.* Lovely had worked on plenty of personal injury cases, too. Skimming the correspondence between Pierce and his client, he could see they were overstating the extent of the latter's disability. Were there any honest people left in the world? He went for the next file. Oz was still opening and closing desk drawers. The sound stopped suddenly. Lovely glanced up.

"Gun," Oz said quietly.

The hairs on the back of Lovely's neck stood up. He dropped the file and crossed the room. A stainless-steel automatic was lying in Pierce's bottom drawer. Lovely picked it up between his thumb and forefinger. A North American Guardian, .32 caliber. The slight discoloration on the trigger meant it had been fired many times. Lovely removed the clip. It was full, and there was a cartridge in the chamber. He and Oz exchanged grim glances. As Lovely was sliding the clip back into place, the deadbolt in the reception area door clicked open.

Oz lunged for the light switch, plunging the room into darkness. He ducked behind the open door. Lovely dropped to the floor and backed into the kneehole of Pierce's desk. His head was jammed against the underside of the drawer. The reception area door opened and closed. Was it Pierce? Footsteps came across the carpeted floor. They stopped at the entrance to the office. A flashlight switched on, and its beam swept over the room. A security guard, Lovely guessed. The person stood in the doorway for a minute, then switched off his light. Lovely let out his breath. The footsteps moved away, and he heard the person check the door to David's office. It was locked. Silence followed.

Lovely felt a cold sensation seep into him. Was the guard wondering why Pierce and Kantor had left one office locked and the other wide open? The footsteps came back. The flashlight beam swept over the room again. Then the overhead light turned on. Lovely listened to the person walk across the office and come around the corner of the desk. An instant later, Oz had the intruder face-first against the wall with his arm twisted behind his back. It was a uniformed guard with nightstick on his belt.

"Take it easy," the guard grunted. "I ain't even armed."

The voice sent a jolt through Lovely's body.

"Tie him up with tape from the desk," Oz said.

Lovely heaved a miserable sigh. "Let him go."

"What?!"

"I can't tie him up, I know him."

"Oh, shit."

Oz let the man go, and Lovely came out from under the desk.

The guard turned to look at him. "Oh, Jesus!" he gasped. "Max Lovely!"

"Hi, Jack."

There *was* one honest person left in the world: Sergeant Jack Motherwell, who had served twenty-eight years on the Boston Police until a bullet in the hip forced him into early retirement. Motherwell was such a martinet that a wise-cracking Lieutenant had dubbed him "Mother May I."

Motherwell spotted Pierce's automatic lying on the floor behind the desk.

"Jesus, Mary, and Joseph," he whispered. "And you were always so clean." He picked up the gun in a handkerchief and pocketed it.

"It's not the way it looks," Lovely said.

"Maybe not, but it's bad enough. You know I got to turn you in, Max." He looked at Oz and shook his head.

"Check out these threads," Oz protested. "Do I look like a criminal?"

"I ain't laughing." Motherwell picked up Pierce's phone.

"Wait!" Lovely said.

Motherwell shook his head. "You know I can't play no

favorites, Max. I got to call the police." He started dialing.

"Just give me five minutes to explain," Lovely said. "This lawyer may have attempted murder."

Motherwell glanced at him sharply. "Allen Pierce?"

Lovely nodded. "That's his gun. His partner's missing."

"David Kantor?"

Lovely nodded again. "Kantor's wife hired me."

Motherwell eyed him for a moment. Then he put down the phone. "I'll listen."

CHAPTER NINE

It was almost ten p.m. when Lovely walked into his house. Jack Motherwell hadn't turned them over to the police.

"For a minute I thought you were a burglar," he had said to Lovely. "But I know you ain't a liar." Then he turned to Oz and said, "If you ain't a criminal, how come you can pick locks?"

"My father was a locksmith."

"And you?"

"A mason, but I take lock work when it comes my way."

That seemed to please Motherwell. "Coupla amateurs," he said. "Don't even know enough to keep the lights off when you're burglaring an office. Pierce walked out half an hour ago, so I wondered when I saw light coming under his door."

Oz winked at Lovely, who cleared his throat. "Listen, Jack, how about giving us an hour to, ah, finish up in here?"

"Don't even *think* about it! Put everything back and lock everything up. And I want you both to swear you won't try this again. You got to play by the rules, Max. When you have enough evidence for a warrant, you can go to the police."

That was how it ended. With his underhanded options reduced, Lovely would have to try the direct frontal approach: tomorrow morning, he'd pay Pierce a visit.

The phone rang and he picked it up.

"Hi, Max, it's Ralph Henman. I have a favor to ask."

Lovely groaned silently. *Here we go again.*

"Brigitte and I are leaving on vacation this Friday. We were wondering if Cyrus could stay with you while we're away."

Lovely cleared his throat. "Nice of you to think of me,

Ralph, but I'm hardly ever around the house these days. I'm sure Cyrus would be happier with someone who could spend more time with him."

"No, no! He likes you best. You're the only one he doesn't hiss at."

"Uh, look, Ralph, I'm sorry, but I have too much going on to take care of people's cats."

"Come on, Max. It's only for a week."

"Then send him to the kennel."

"Max! How can you say that?! They'll put him in a cage, for God's sake."

"So have one of those pet sitters take care of him, or leave him with somebody else."

"You're the only one he gets along with. You know how Cyrus is—he won't eat if he's around people he doesn't like."

"He'll eat when he gets hungry enough."

"Please, Max. He's a very sensitive cat. You don't want him getting sick or dying or something, do you?"

Lovely sighed. "Look, Ralph, if you absolutely can't find anyone else, I suppose I might consider it. But only as a last resort, all right?"

"All right. Thanks."

Lovely put down the phone and shook his head. That's how he had wound up with the gar. A friend leaving on a two-month trip to South America had persuaded Lovely to take care of it.

"And by the way," the friend had said, once the aquarium was installed in Lovely's room, "it only eats live guppies."

Lovely pulled off his clothes and left them in a heap on his bedroom floor. He crawled into bed and fell asleep before he had time to turn out the light.

In his dream, he was downtown surrounded by tall buildings. Men in suits were walking past. Some carried briefcases, but others carried guns—pistols, rifles, assault weapons. Incredibly, no one seemed to notice. A cat began to meow. The sound turned into the cries of an old woman, then back into a cat.

Lovely woke up. A cat was meowing outside. He glanced at the window. Cyrus was not on the sill. It didn't sound like Cyrus, anyway. It was more high-pitched, like a kitten. Odd; none of his neighbors had a kitten as far as he knew. He checked the clock. One-forty. He threw on his robe and went out the back door.

The night had grown cool. He could feel dew-soaked grass beneath his bare feet. Thin clouds moved across a sliver of moon. The meowing seemed to be coming from the maple tree outside his bedroom window. As he neared the tree, the sound stopped. A cricket chirped, but everything else was silent. Lovely squinted up into the branches. He should have brought a flashlight. Something rustled behind him. He glanced over his shoulder. A tall figure stepped out from the yew trees.

Lovely dived for the ground. He heard the muffled report of a silencer and the pop of a bullet passing over his head. He scrambled toward the tree. Two more shots came in quick succession, one glancing off the trunk, showering him with shards of bark. He cut in behind the tree, then rose to his feet and ran, keeping the trunk between himself and the gunman. He heard another pop and one of Mrs. Grybowski's windows shattered. A second thudded into the window sill just to his right. Lovely was running straight toward her house. He would have to cut left or right, taking him out of the cover of the tree. He cut left. Too late, he saw that the prowler had anticipated him and was angling toward him, cutting him off. Lovely stopped short. The prowler dropped into a crouch and took aim. He was barely fifteen feet away. He fired. Lovely heard a click but saw no muzzle flash. The prowler fired again. Nothing happened. Lovely's knees almost gave out. Either the gun was a five-shot revolver, or it was an automatic that had jammed. Lovely couldn't see which in the darkness; nor could he make out the man's face.

Something flashed in the prowler's hand. A knife. The prowler stood up and shoved the gun into the waistband of his pants. Lovely tightened the belt of his robe. At least he'd have a chance.

The prowler stood on the balls of his feet, watching Lovely, waiting or hesitating— Lovely couldn't tell which. Then he charged. Lovely braced himself. The prowler stopped short. He backed away and circled right. Lovely followed, eyes on the knife.

A light blinked on above them. Someone threw open a window with a loud scrape.

"What in Sam hell's going on out there?!" a man's voice bellowed. It was Mrs. Grybowski's landlord.

"Grab your shotgun and come out," Lovely shouted. "We got a prowler."

The prowler hesitated for a moment. Then he turned and fled. Lovely watched him go, wondering where the cat sound had come from.

CHAPTER TEN

Lovely took his Ruger .357 Magnum from the closet and released the cylinder. Fully loaded. He slid the gun into his shoulder holster. And this was supposed to be the day he met the good guys.

It had been another late night, telling his story to the police and taping up Mrs. Grybowski's window. The cat sound, it turned out, had been produced by a small speaker and miniature receiver set in the maple tree. The prowler must have operated the transmitter by hand from his hiding place in the yews. Obviously, the man had some knowledge of electronics, which made him that much more dangerous. Even more disturbing was the fact that he knew Lovely would come outside to save a cat.

Lovely took a gold ring out of his desk and slipped it on the ring finger of his right hand. The week before, he had installed a safety device on his gun. It would not fire unless the shooter wore the magnetic ring. This would prevent Lovely's little nephews from putting holes in each other when they came to visit. Also, it reduced the chance that someone would shoot Lovely with his own gun.

Lovely fiddled with the ring, trying to make it feel less annoying. He wasn't in the habit of wearing jewelry. He'd give it a few more days. If he couldn't tolerate it, he'd use his spare gun instead.

The phone rang and he picked it up.

"My name is Judy Winter," the caller said. She spoke with a slight southern accent. "Irene Freeman at the Women's Crisis Center gave me your name. I'm having a problem with a stalker."

"Sorry to hear that. You know who it is?"

"No, never saw him until a few weeks ago."

"What does he do?"

"Follows me and watches me. I'll be getting into my car or walking down the street, and suddenly, there he'll be."

There was a barely-controlled intensity to her voice that was unsettling. Lovely imagined her leaning forward in her chair, fists clenched.

"Does he approach you?"

"No, but the way he leers at me—it's sick. It scares me."

"Did you talk to the police?"

"Yes, but they can't help me because he always walks away, if I go inside or take out my cell phone. I don't know what to do. I'm frightened all the time, now, afraid he's going to catch me alone in the street some night..." Her voice cracked.

"I'm sorry. That kind of thing would terrify anyone."

"Irene said you'd help me. I was hoping you could spend a few days with me, sort of watching me from a distance, and maybe you could catch him or follow him, and find out who he is."

Lovely could feel his resistance. He gave her a response that was honest, if incomplete.

"I'm tied up with another case. The earliest I could do it would be next week."

"Next week! But he's watching me everyday!"

"I'm very sorry, but there's just no way I could help you right now. Irene knows some other private investigators."

"She does?"

"Sure."

"Well, all right. I'll ask if anyone's available. If not, you'll help me next week?"

Lovely hesitated. "Yes."

"Ok. Thanks."

He put down the phone. She sounded like a ticking bomb. Let her find someone else.

Lovely went out the front door and a gust of wind nearly blew him back inside. The temperature had dropped twenty degrees during the night and the sky was overcast. He climbed into his battered Chrysler and headed downtown.

A hard wind blew from his left, making a whistling noise in the gap between the window and the old convertible top. Lovely cast a glance at the threatening sky. When it rained, water dripped in through a frayed spot in the canvas, gradually soaking the left sleeve of whatever he was wearing. It wasn't the car's only inconvenient quirk. During cold spells, the drafty cab never warmed up enough for Lovely to remove his hat and gloves; and during heat waves, the black canvas top turned the interior into an oven. But those mild sunny days and warm nights, when Lovely put down the top and drove along the coast smelling the ocean, made it all worthwhile.

The color rose to Marcia Paige's cheeks when Lovely walked into the reception area of Pierce and Kantor. He could see that the door to Pierce's office was open. Lovely winked at her.

"I'd like to see Mr. Pierce, please. My name's Max Lovely. I was here yesterday."

"One moment, please." She picked up the phone and spoke briefly to Pierce. "I'm afraid Mr. Pierce is busy. He won't be able to see you today."

"That's what he thinks." Lovely walked past Marcia's desk and into Pierce's office. He closed the door behind him.

Pierce had a document spread out in front of him and a pen in his hand. He glanced up at Lovely without expression. Lovely removed his jacket, revealing his Ruger—just in case Pierce had a mind to reach into the bottom drawer of his desk. Lovely sat down in the leather chair.

"I spoke to a lot of people yesterday," he said, "and everyone's worried about David. Everyone except you. That got me wondering. So I asked around about how you and David get along. You told me you get along fine, but everyone else says you two can't stand each other. That makes you a liar, which is not a good thing in my book. Then I find out there's a bullet hole in David's car door. I'd like to know how it got there."

Pierce's expression was still blank. He laid down his

pen and leaned forward across his desk. "I'm not afraid of you. But if you had any sense, you'd be afraid of me: scared to death. Get out of my office."

They stared at each other in silence for a minute. Then Lovely stood up and put on his jacket. The conference table by the window was still covered with the neat stacks of papers he had seen the night before.

"The air in here's rotten," he said. He threw open the window, letting in a blast of cold wind. He walked to the door and looked back. The room was filled with flying papers, like a flock of pigeons startled by a cat.

CHAPTER ELEVEN

Eliot pulled up in front of the Greenhouse apartment building on Huntington Avenue and beeped his horn. Anthony "the Ant" Diaz came out of the lobby. He wore a camouflage windbreaker, camouflage pants, and combat boots. He had shoulder-length hair, bushy eyebrows, and a big, droopy moustache which made him appear to be scowling, even on those occasions when he was not. The Ant only came up to Eliot's shoulder, but he had countered this deficiency by increasing his girth. He weighed two hundred pounds and could bench press twice his body weight. He looked, Eliot decided, like a very muscular walrus, dressed for battle, who had woken up on the wrong side of the ice floe.

The Ant climbed into the front seat of Eliot's Lexus SUV. "Morning, Ellis," he said. He had a deep voice and spoke slowly and deliberately.

"It's `Eliot,'" Eliot said amiably.

The Ant turned his shaggy face toward him. "That's what I said."

Eliot swallowed. "Sorry."

They drove around the block to Jaimee Kantor's, rang the buzzer, and went up. Jaimee opened the apartment door and smiled. Eliot's knees almost gave out. *Holy moley.* He could feel his armpits getting damp.

"You came for the keys?" Jaimee suggested.

"Uh, yeah."

Her eyes drifted past him to the Ant.

"Oh, this is Anthony. He's...with me."

She gave Eliot the keys, and he walked down the stairs and out the front door. He couldn't remember if he had thanked her.

They went around the corner to West Canton Street, leaning into the wind. Trees shaded the narrow, quiet lane. Victorian townhouses, five stories high, lined the block on both sides. Although a century and a half old, most had crisply pointed brick work and bright brass hardware on the entrance doors. Azaleas and lilacs bloomed in the twelve-foot-square front yards. Eliot and the Ant climbed the tall stone steps in front of David's townhouse. The Ant paused, looking down the street.

"What?" Eliot said. "Is everything ok?"

"Let's go in."

Eliot unlocked the door and hurried inside. He glanced around the carpeted hallway. A stair with a carved mahogany newel post and banister led up to the second floor. A pair of mailboxes hung on the wall, and beside them, a door with a brass number one. The door opened and a woman looked out.

"Oh!" she said. She glanced from Eliot to the Ant. "You're not the mailman."

"No," Eliot agreed.

She went back inside. A moment later, she opened the door again. "I don't mean to be nosy, but there's only one other person living in this building, and you're not him."

Eliot smiled. "I understand." He handed her his card. "We were hired by Jaimee Kantor. You can call her if you want to check up on us."

That satisfied her, and she went back inside. Eliot and the Ant climbed a flight of stairs and entered David's three-story condominium. They found the file cabinet in the den off the master bedroom. The drawers were open—and empty.

"Oh-oh," Eliot said.

"Max told you it was full?"

"Yeah."

"Come on."

Eliot followed him out of the building. The Ant paused at the top of the stone steps and looked down the street.

"This way," he said.

Reluctantly, Eliot followed.

The Ant walked up to a parked Ford Explorer and

stuck his head in the passenger's window. A young man with a puffy face and red cheeks sat behind the wheel. He filled the front seat the way Eliot would have filled an MG Midget.

"You know the feeling someone's watching you?" the Ant said to the man. "Well, I just had it, and the someone was you."

"I don't even know who you ah," the man said in a heavy Boston accent.

"Maybe not, but you were watching me."

The man turned and spat out his window. "So what ah you gonna do about it?"

"I don't know," the Ant said. "Let's talk." He opened the door and hopped in the passenger's seat.

The man gaped at him. "What the fuck ah you doin'?!"

"Power seats," the Ant said. "I like these." He pushed the button to recline.

"I can't believe this shit! Who *ah* you?"

The Ant reclined his seat all the way, so he was staring at the ceiling. "Now I feel like I'm in a rocket ship."

"Listen," the man said. "If you don't get out of my cah, I sweah I'm gonna staht swingin'."

"Ok." The Ant grabbed a pad of paper off the console and hopped out.

"Hey!" the man shouted. "Gimme that!"

The Ant slipped it in his pocket. "Come and get it."

The man jumped out his door and ran around the front of the car. The Ant went around the back.

"Gimme that or I'll beat you to a fuckin' pulp!"

"You gotta catch me, first."

Eliot retreated down the sidewalk.

The Ant ran the man around the car—two laps, three, four. The man was breathing hard and his face looked like it was sunburned, but he was gaining on the Ant. He was over six feet tall, and had to weigh two-fifty. Eliot ducked between a parked van and an SUV. What would he do if the man tackled the Ant? Eliot hadn't been in a fight since eighth grade.

The man was barely two paces behind the Ant, now, towering over him like a grizzly. Eliot glanced around, wondering if he should call the police. Then the Ant cut sideways and ran down the sidewalk toward Eliot's hiding place. Eliot froze. Directly in front of him, the Ant dropped to his knees. The man went flying over him. When Eliot peered out from behind the van, the man was face-down on the sidewalk with the Ant on his back. The Ant had the man's arms crossed behind him, and he was pulling the man's wrists outward, bending his shoulders back and lifting his head off the concrete.

"Bet you never saw this hold," the Ant said to his victim. "Made it up myself. Call it the `criss-cross-crush.' Pretty good, huh?"

The man was gasping.

The Ant looked over his shoulder at Eliot and grinned. "Take the pad out of my pocket."

Eliot hesitated.

"Don't worry," the Ant said, "he can't hurt you."

Eliot edged out from behind the van. As he neared the Ant, the man began to struggle.

"Cut it out," the Ant growled. "Do I have to snap your spine to keep you still?"

The man stopped struggling.

Eliot yanked the pad out of the Ant's pocket and backed away. It had David's address on it, and beneath it, a phone number with the South Shore area code.

"Take this guy's cell phone from his pocket," the Ant said, "call the number and see what you get."

Eliot hesitated.

"Move!" the Ant growled.

Eliot felt the man's pockets, found a cell phone, wriggled it loose, backed quickly away. He dialed the number with trembling fingers.

"It's Lou," a man said.

Eliot hung up and reported this to the Ant.

"Now check the back of the truck for the files," the Ant instructed.

Eliot ran to the SUV and stuck his face in the back window.

"Nothing!"

"Ok, we can go." The Ant gave the man's arms a yank. "I'm going to get up, and you're going to lay here and count to a hundred. I got a Heckler and Koch nine holstered under my arm, so don't count too fast. And if you follow us, I'll pin you again, and this time I *will* snap your spine."

What made Eliot feel slightly sick is that he knew the Ant would do it.

The Ant yanked on the man's arms again. "Got it straight?"

The man nodded.

The Ant looked over his shoulder at Eliot. "Run around the corner. I'll meet you."

Eliot ran.

CHAPTER TWELVE

Eliot and the Ant were headed southbound on the Expressway in Eliot's Lexus. Off to the left, Dorchester Bay looked leaden under the cloudy sky. The Ant sat in the passenger's seat, riding with his head out the window like the golden retriever Eliot had been raised with as a boy. Cold wind blew in and swirled around the cab. Eliot zipped up his jacket.

The Ant had placed a call to a friend at the FBI. The phone number on the pad belonged to a man named Lou Brenna, a made member of the Vermino crime family. Brenna owned a drywall company and a night club, and was active in loan-sharking. He was also the prime suspect in half a dozen unsolved murders stretching back over a decade. He lived in Randolph, an affluent suburb on the South Shore, and operated out of his home.

"You're driving pretty slow," the Ant observed without turning from the window.

Eliot forced his foot down on the accelerator.

Eight miles to the south, they left the highway and wound through the streets of Randolph, past large post-war homes, which looked like they might have been ordered from the same catalog. The town seemed deserted. After four years of living in the city, Eliot had forgotten how empty these bedroom communities could appear on an overcast weekday morning.

The Lexus's dashboard clock said 10:05 when they drove past Brenna's house for the first time. He lived in a huge white garrison, set back from the road on a wooded lot. Eliot could see smoke rising from the chimney.

"Pull over," the Ant said. "We passed a coffee shop a

quarter mile back. Wait for me there. If I don't show by eleven, call my friend at the FBI." He wrote down the man's name and number and handed it to Eliot.

"Don't you think it would be better to wait and go in with Max?" Eliot asked.

The Ant shook his head. "He wouldn't let me do things my way."

Something in how the Ant said "my way" made Eliot's stomach feel fluttery.

The Ant removed his Heckler and Koch automatic and stashed it under his seat.

"You're going without your gun?" Eliot gasped.

"He'd just take it away before letting me in—the kid will have called him. This way, he'll only have one gun instead of two." The Ant climbed out and lumbered back toward Brenna's house.

Eliot shook his head, U-turned, and drove away.

The Ant walked up the long driveway and climbed the three steps to the front portico. He rang the bell. A man opened the door. He was fortyish, medium height, solidly built but not bulky. He was wearing gray flannel trousers and a white button-down shirt with French cuffs. He looked the Ant over.

"Know who I am?" the Ant asked.

"Got an idea. What do you want?"

"If you're Lou Brenna, I want to talk."

"Then talk."

"Can I come in?"

Brenna paused. "I'll have to pat you down."

"Go ahead."

Brenna searched him, then stepped back, holding the door open. He gripped a small automatic in his hand. Even so, he kept some distance between himself and the Ant. He directed his guest to the living room. It could have accommodated the Ant's entire apartment with room to spare. The floor was paved with marble, partially covered by a thick Oriental rug, and the walls were mirrored. A chandelier hung from the ceiling. One corner of the room was taken up by a sectional sofa arranged in an L and a glass coffee table. Logs burned in the fireplace. The crystals of the chandelier flashed yellow and orange in the firelight.

"Have a seat," Brenna said, indicating the sofa.

"That's all right. Always feel safer standing up."

"What's your name?"

"Gomez." The Ant had an obnoxious brother-in-law by that name.

"Gomez what?"

"Just Gomez, till I know you better."

"What were you doing this morning?"

"Looking for David Kantor."

"Why?"

"Because he's missing, and people are getting worried."

"What people?"

Brenna spoke very rapidly. It was a practice which annoyed the Ant because it made his own sluggish speech sound like a record played at half speed. He responded by slowing down even further.

"Can't say. They got to remain... What's the word?"

"I don't know what you're talking about," Brenna snapped.

"Anonymous, that's it. Clients don't get named."

"Clients? You're a private detective?"

"A bodyguard, actually. I got brought in to help."

"That kid you were with is a fucking detective?"

"Well, no, I guess he's kind of a trainee."

"So who the fuck are you working for?"

Not only did this wiseguy talk too fast, he was bossy as hell. Guns did that to people.

"I think the guy would prefer I didn't give his name," the Ant said, "seeing as you're a mobster and all. Now it's my turn to ask some questions. Why are you staking out Kantor's apartment?"

Brenna pointed the automatic at the Ant's chest. "I'm not answering any questions. We're going out to the garage. Turn around and walk through that door."

"But I just got here," the Ant protested. "We hardly even talked yet."

"Move."

The Ant folded his arms across his chest. "Nope."

"What do you mean, nope?! You're nothing to me, Gomez. I'll whack you like stepping on a roach."

"And get my blood all over your house?" The Ant shook his head. "If I don't walk out of here in half an hour, my friends at the FBI are going to come looking for me—they're the ones who told me where you live. You'll never get the place cleaned up in time."

Brenna eyed him for a minute. Then he side-stepped over to the fireplace and pulled out a hot poker. "Move, or I'll brand your ass. That won't spill any blood. Through that door and down the hall."

The Ant looked at a spot on the wall behind Brenna and snapped his eyes open in surprise. Brenna glanced over his shoulder. The Ant stepped forward and drove the steel toe of his combat boot into Brenna's right wrist. The impact made a sound like a branch breaking. The gun flew out of Brenna's hand and he went down, clutching his wrist.

The Ant grinned. "An old trick my brother used to pull on me in snowball fights. Must'a fell for it a hundred times." He picked up the fallen gun and slipped it into his pocket. Now Brenna wouldn't be so bossy. "Broken wrist hurts like a bitch, doesn't it? Did that in third grade falling off my bike. Couldn't go swimming for six weeks."

Brenna didn't respond. He was breathing like an asthmatic.

The Ant said, "I got a few easy questions—easy as long as you answer them, anyway. Why are you watching David Kantor?"

Brenna didn't say anything. He didn't seem to be paying attention.

The Ant noticed a spiral of smoke rising up from the floor. The fireplace poker had fallen on the Oriental carpet. He went over and picked it up.

"Jeez," he said. "Sorry about that hole in your rug." He

touched the end of the poker. "Whoa, this baby's still hot." One of Brenna's pant legs was pulled up. The Ant laid the poker on his calf. "See?"

Brenna screamed and jerked his leg away. "All right," he gasped. He took a few deep breaths. "I was told to get rid of him." He was speaking through clenched teeth.

"What'd he do?"

"I have no idea."

The Ant raised the poker.

"I swear I don't know! I never heard of him before. He's no one in our organization."

"Did you shoot at him a few weeks ago?"

"No. Someone else tried and fucked up, and it got handed to me."

"What did you do with David's files?" the Ant asked.

"Files?"

"The ones missing from the file cabinet in his apartment."

"Don't know nothing about that."

The Ant nodded. "Those are all my questions. Easy, just like I said." He tossed the poker in the fireplace and left.

Eliot was standing by the coffee shop window when the Ant came into view. Eliot hurried outside and went down the road to meet him. The Ant was beaming.

"I guess you're ok, huh?" Eliot said.

"Sure."

"You got the information?"

"Yeah." The Ant told him what he had found out.

Eliot thought about asking how he had induced Brenna to talk, but decided he didn't want to know. He was feeling a little queasy. They climbed into the Lexus and headed back toward Boston. They rode in silence, the Ant with his head out the window. The only other vehicle in the northbound lane was an oil truck thirty yards ahead of them, belching black smoke. Diesel fumes were coming in through the Ant's open window. Eliot backed off the gas. The smell was making him sick.

When they crossed a bridge over the Neponset River, the Ant took Brenna's automatic out of his pocket and threw it, frisbee-like, into the water. A mile down the road, he turned away from the window and leaned back in his seat.

"You know," he said thoughtfully, "those Mafia guys always think they're so tough. But their bones snap just like anyone else's."

Eliot pulled over, opened his door, and threw up.

CHAPTER THIRTEEN

A grassy park occupied the center of Louisburg Square, shaded by elms and honey locusts, the latter in bloom, and surrounded by a wrought-iron fence. Matching rows of brick townhouses dating from the 1840's overlooked the park. Louisa May Alcott had lived at Number Ten Louisburg Square, and Jenny Lind, the Swedish Nightingale, had married her accompanist at Number Twenty. David Kantor's lender, Andrew Winthrop, lived three doors down from the Alcott house in a four-and-a-half story bowfront with a shallow, Corinthian-columned portico. Lovely could see a lone doorbell on the entrance, indicating the building was still a single-family residence. Most of Boston's townhouses had long since been converted to condominiums. Lovely rang the bell, waited, tried again. No one came.

The wind had died down and the cloud cover was breaking up. Lovely took a seat on the grass in a sunny corner of the park and leaned back against the iron fence. Winthrop's phone number was unlisted and Jaimee didn't know it, but he would have to come home sooner or later. Lovely closed his eyes and settled into the present.

It wasn't an easy place to stay. The mind tended to project itself into the future—plans, decisions, anticipation—or dwell upon the past. The present was much more unstable. It never held still long enough for one to grasp it, and yet it was always right there. When the mind did manage to remain in the present, the experience wasn't necessarily blissful. But when Lovely opened to the experience, the clutter and distraction drained from his consciousness, and he became intensely aware of everything around him and within him. Over the years, this awareness had become a permanent part of his psyche. From it flowed his extraordinary perceptiveness. Unfortunately, feeling everything so acutely had its disadvantages. As a boy, he had never thought twice about decking a bully. Now there were days he couldn't swat a mosquito.

Lovely heard voices and opened one eye. Two men in suits descended the front steps of a townhouse and headed down the street. They looked at him with a combination of curiosity and suspicion.

"I'm the fool on the hill," Lovely said. But they weren't listening.

An hour later, a charcoal-gray Jaguar sedan pulled up in front of Winthrop's house. A man with a briefcase climbed out and let himself into the building. Lovely waited five minutes then crossed the street and rang the bell. The man came to the door. He was half a foot shorter than Lovely, flabby, with sandy hair and a good tan. Lovely introduced himself and handed the man his card. He was always interested to see how people reacted when they learned he was a PI. The most common responses were fear, guilt, or excited curiosity. Winthrop looked concerned—a response Lovely had never seen—and his concern had a stiffness to it.

"Are you Mr. Andrew Winthrop?" Lovely asked.

"Yes. What's this regarding?"

"I was hired by David Kantor's wife. She's worried about his absence. Can I ask you a few questions?"

"Of course."

Winthrop ushered him into the house. They passed through the entrance hall and into the front parlor. Heavy, burgundy-colored drapes framed the tall front windows. A fringed velvet swag of the same color covered the mantel. Facing it was a mahogany sofa with spiral arms and lion's-paw feet, upholstered in silk damask. A portrait of a man in tails and a top hat frowned down from the wall. A Winthrop ancestor, no doubt. Two massive sliding oak doors separated the front parlor from the rear parlor, or drawing room. The doors were half open, and through them, Lovely could glimpse modernity: a desk with a computer, a conference table, a copier.

Winthrop directed Lovely to the sofa and seated himself on a carved rosewood chair. "This is worrisome—Jaimee hiring a private investigator. I thought David was on vacation."

"He may be, but no one has heard from him since he left. Have you?"

Winthrop shook his head. "I hope Jaimee doesn't have reason to think some harm has come to him."

"No, she's just concerned about how long it's been."

"I don't blame her."

Winthrop's comments were reasonable and didn't exactly sound untrue, but they had an unnatural ring.

"I understand you hold most of his mortgages," Lovely said.

"That's right."

"Is he behind on any of his payments?"

"No. He's not in financial trouble with me."

"Have you received any payments from him since he left?"

"Not from David himself. A management company collects the rents and pays the bills."

Lovely paused. He couldn't shake the feeling that something was wrong with Winthrop's responses. They sounded...rehearsed.

"Have you spoken to Roland Moore in the last forty-eight hours?" Lovely asked.

Winthrop blinked. "No." It was the first word he had uttered which sounded sincere.

"Then how did you know I was coming?"

Winthrop's mouth opened a good half-inch, and the color rose to his face. "I didn't!"

Lovely felt a twinge of empathetic embarrassment at the obvious falseness of the denial, followed by irritation for having to feel the embarrassment.

"The clerk at the registry of deeds told my assistant someone was looking up David's properties," Lovely said. He let the statement hang for a few seconds. "I haven't asked the clerk for a description of the man—yet."

Winthrop hesitated. "It was me."

"Wondering if David had any secret condos to hide out in?"

Winthrop's mouth tightened. He sat up straight on the couch. "I have five-point-two million loaned out to David Kantor. I have every reason to want to know where he is. I was also concerned he could have gotten into financial trouble with a project I was unaware of."

"What did you find out?"

"Nothing I didn't already know."

"I recall seeing two properties financed by Century Bank," Lovely said.

"That is correct. I knew about them."

A phone rang in the rear parlor. There was a beep and a man's voice came on. "Hi, Andrew, it's Keith Riordan..."

Winthrop leaped to his feet and hurried into the other room.

"I'm in my office," the caller continued. "Give me a..."

Winthrop punched a button, cutting off Riordan's voice. He returned to his chair.

"I'm impressed," Lovely said. "Mayor Riordan's a friend of yours?"

"Just an old classmate—I do some fundraising for him. You asked about the properties financed with Century: I know some people over there, so I checked on the loans. They're up to date."

Winthrop's affected concern was gone now, replaced by an irritable contempt which was obviously no act. He seemed very accustomed to it. It had to be tough being a Winthrop, even a bogus one. Day in and day out, he was forced to rub elbows with nouveau-riche neighbors, Irish and Jewish lawyers, cab drivers with foreign accents... And now, Lovely.

"What do you know about Allen Pierce?" Lovely asked.

"He's from an old family," Winthrop replied. "He graduated three years ahead of me at Choate."

"Is he an honest and decent man?"

"I would assume so." He glanced at his watch.

"What about Roland Moore?"

"I wouldn't have lent money to David if I didn't believe his partner to be trustworthy." Winthrop rose to his feet. "I'm afraid I've given you all the time I can spare. Good luck with your search."

Lovely descended the steps in front of Winthrop's house and headed down the cobblestone street. What the hell was going on? Winthrop had been expecting him, but how was that possible? Jaimee was the only person who knew about the visit, and she had nothing to gain by whispering behind Lovely's back. And why had Winthrop hesitated before acknowledging his visit to the registry of deeds, when his explanation was perfectly reasonable? What did he have to hide? Then there was the call from Mayor Riordan. Winthrop had flown out of his chair to cut the sound and then changed the subject. Why didn't he want Lovely to associate him with the Mayor? The unanswered questions were piling up.

At the foot of Beacon Hill, Lovely turned onto Charles Street, passing the Charles Street Meeting House where Frederick Douglass and William Lloyd Garrison had spoken out against slavery in the decades before the Civil War. By then, no doubt, Andrew Winthrop's ancestors had slipped quietly out of the slave trade and joined the abolitionist cause. A Boston *Globe* newspaper box with a headline about the Mayor caught Lovely's eye. He bought a copy of the paper and drove home to Watertown.

On the way, the Ant called. Lovely listened with steadily growing amazement while the Ant plodded through his story. The Ant described in detail how he and Eliot had borrowed the red-faced man's pad and cell phone, but he was vague about what had happened inside Lou Brenna's house. Lovely decided not to press for details.

"Suddenly this whole thing is looking very ugly," Lovely said.

"Yeah."

"If Brenna has instructions to kill David, do they have to come from Vermino?"

"Sure, they don't whack people without approval from the top."

"God. I wonder what David did."

"Only one person to ask."

Lovely grimaced. Alessandro Vermino had earned the sobriquet *L'Impaziente* by murdering the aging Don who had preceded him, along with six of the Don's inner circle. Unlike most Mafia bosses, Vermino still carried out some of his own hits. Apparently, he enjoyed it.

Lovely said, "Three guys have lied to me in the past twenty-four hours, and two were lawyers." He briefly recounted his meetings with Moore, Pierce, and Winthrop. "Do you know who represents Vermino in court?"

"No, but I got a friend at the FBI who will."

"While you're talking to him, find out if there's a place I can ask Vermino a few questions without being gunned down by his bodyguards."

Lovely's next call was to Eliot.

"I wasn't very smooth in front of Jaimee this morning," Eliot said. "Just warning you, in case she complains about paying three hundred a day for a guy who can't speak in complete sentences."

Lovely laughed. "From what the Ant tells me, you earned your pay."

"Not really. Did he tell you about the file cabinet?"

"Yeah. You sure you checked the right one—a black, two-drawer job in the den off the master bedroom?"

"Yup. It's the only one in the apartment."

"It was full yesterday."

"It was empty today."

"Makes you wonder if they knew you were coming."

"Who's `they'?" Eliot asked.

"I have no idea. The Ant says Brenna knew nothing about the files."

"We met the woman who lives below David. Maybe she saw the person who took them. The name on her mailbox was C. Shearson. I wrote it down."

"Attaboy. Like I said, you earned your pay."

Lovely looked up C. Shearson in the phone book, called, and arranged to meet with her that evening. Ten minutes later, the Ant called back.

"For as long as anyone can remember, the Verminos have been represented by a lawyer named Aaron Zimmer, of Zimmer and Zimmer on Court Street. He's in business with his son, Jeffrey."

"Oh, yeah," Lovely said. "I remember seeing his name in the paper when Vermino was on trial a few years back." Zimmer had succeeded in getting him acquitted of racketeering charges.

"I also asked about David Kantor, Allen Pierce, Roland Moore, and Andrew Winthrop. The FBI never heard of them."

"How about a place to run into Vermino?"

"He plays golf at the South Hills Country Club almost every afternoon. Tees off around five. He's trying to fit in at the Club, so he never brings a bodyguard. Usually plays in a foursome with other members."

"Thanks, I'll see if I can get a word with him between putts."

Lovely hung up. He thought of the prowler showing up while he was at Jaimee's, and knowing he would come outside to save a cat; of Winthrop expecting his visit, and now the files removed. It gave him the unsettling feeling he was being watched.

CHAPTER FOURTEEN

Lovely leaned back in his chair, put his feet up on his desk, and unfolded the copy of the *Globe* he had bought on Charles Street.

"Mayor Says No to Governor Race," the headline said. "At a press conference today, Democratic Mayor Keith Riordan dismissed rumors that he would run for governor against Republican incumbent Lawrence Aldrich. `I'm committed to my party, and of course I'd like to see a Democrat in the State House. But my first responsibility is to the people of Boston, and I feel I can best serve them as Mayor.'"

In other words, Aldrich would beat him like a drum. The economy was strong, the Governor had approval ratings in the high sixties, and the state's Republican Party could back him up with mountains of cash. Even a Kennedy would be hard-pressed to unseat him.

The article quoted a Democratic leader who expressed hope Riordan would change his mind. "He's our best chance for mounting a challenge to Aldrich, and the deadline for entering the Democratic primary is still a month away." Another Democrat extolled the Mayor's record and qualifications. He had been a Fulbright scholar and made *Law Review* at Harvard. After graduating, he taught political science at Boston University. He had been a member of the Boston School Committee and served on the City Council before being elected mayor. He had been re-elected two years ago by the largest margin the city had seen since the reign of James Michael Curley.

Lovely remembered Riordan's first run. His opponent, the incumbent mayor, was a big family-values man, married, with three children. The incumbent led in the polls until voters learned about his dalliance with a seventeen-year-old. The enterprising young woman had secretly videotaped one of their trysts and sold the film to an internet smut dealer. Riordan did a convincing job of not looking gleeful when the scandal broke.

Lovely turned to page two of the *Globe*. In another article, a Democratic state senator criticized Aldrich for his planned hunting trip to Georgia, scheduled for the last week of May. "Every year, the Governor goes to Georgia, when there's plenty of good hunting right here in Massachusetts. The taxpayers of this Commonwealth pay Mr. Aldrich's salary; the least he could do is spend his money here."

Lovely tossed the paper aside. Maybe these dirtbags would hunt each other into extinction. He picked up the phone and called Jaimee.

"I forgot to warn you that Eliot is a bit shy around women."

Jaimee laughed. "He's adorable. Where did you find him?"

"In a cabbage patch. His family's in the cabbage business. But that's not why I called. Mayor Riordan phoned while I was at Andrew Winthrop's house today. I gather they were classmates somewhere. Do you know if Riordan was at Harvard Law at the same time as Andrew and David?"

"Sure, they all graduated in '94. In fact, all three were on *Law Review* together."

"And they're friends?"

"Not close friends, but David always supported Keith in his political campaigns. Two years ago, when David was president of the Chamber of Commerce, he persuaded the group to endorse Keith for mayor."

"All right, that's all I needed for now. I'll be in touch."

Lovely hung up and called City Hall. He made it through to the Mayor's secretary and introduced himself.

"I'm working on a missing-persons case involving a friend of the Mayor. Can I make an appointment to see him?"

"The earliest I could get you in would be the end of next week, and I'd have to clear it with him first."

"That's no good. I need to see him today or tomorrow. Can you tell him it's urgent?"

She hesitated. "Who's the friend?"

"A classmate of his named David Kantor."

"Please hold."

A minute later, the secretary came back on the line. "Mayor Riordan will speak to you now."

Riordan picked up. "I spoke to Andrew Winthrop an hour ago," he said. "He told me no one has heard from David in three weeks and people are beginning to worry. Is there anything I can do?"

Lovely was caught off guard by the Mayor's eagerness to help. "Well, you could start by answering a question about Winthrop. He was quick to downplay his connection to you. Any idea why?"

Riordan chuckled. "Probably because I'm Irish and a Democrat."

"Then why does he support your campaigns?"

"Because through Andrew's eyes, the other candidates look like anarchists and socialists. He's a good man, though. Don't let his aristocratic airs put you off. Did he tell you his family has been in that Louisburg Square house for seven generations?"

"No."

"It's true. The old Winthrop in that painting was ambassador to Great Britain. He used to hunt with King Edward the Seventh. You can't blame Andrew for being a bit snobby—it's in his genes."

"How well do you know David?" Lovely asked.

"We met fifteen years ago in law school. We don't spend much time together these days—we're both so busy— but we keep in touch. He and Andrew have always contributed to my campaigns. I'm very grateful to them."

"Any idea where David might have gone, or why?"

"No."

"What can you tell me about Allen Pierce?" Lovely asked.

"Is that David's law partner?"

"Yes."

"I've never met him."

"How about Roland Moore?"

"I'm not familiar with the name."

Lovely paused, casting about for a question to test Riordan's conscience. "Can you get me in to see the police commissioner?"

"I'm sure I can. Would you like me to arrange that for you?"

"Not yet, thanks. Maybe in a couple days."

"Whenever you're ready."

Lovely heard Riordan's intercom beep. "Senator Donahoe is on line one, Keith."

"I have to take this call," Riordan said. "Just let me know if there's anything else I can do."

Lovely hung up the phone and tossed his pad and pencil onto his desk. When someone lied to him, it was like a sour note. But it wasn't something he heard, it was something he felt—a note which vibrated discordantly in his body. He hadn't felt that during his conversation with Riordan. In fact, he hadn't felt anything at all.

The smell of frying food drifted in through Lovely's window, inducing hunger pangs. He hadn't eaten since breakfast. He went into the kitchen and opened the refrigerator. It was empty except for the contents of the door racks. He muttered an oath. He pulled out the vegetable bin and found one onion and some wilted celery. That gave him an idea. He scrounged around in the cabinet and found a can of tuna. As he carried it to the can opener, he noticed the label with its picture of a smiling fish. He thought of the gar, and the guppies, and the fish he was about to eat. He couldn't do it. It was going to be one of those days.

He put away the tuna and pulled a jar of peanut butter from the refrigerator door. He had no bread, but a search of the kitchen turned up a box of matzoh left over from Passover. The stuff tasted like cardboard when fresh, so an extra few months wouldn't make any difference. With a sigh, he sat down at the table. Not much of a meal, but it was better than

70

feeling guilty. Just barely.

The doorbell rang. Lovely's landlord, Pete Dernakowski, stood on the front porch grinning broadly. He had a sunburned face and curly white hair that hadn't seen a comb recently. He came up to Lovely's chin.

"Went fishing out by Thompson's Island today, Max. Caught some flounder." He held up a serving plate. The fillets were batter-dipped and fried a crispy golden brown. "Piping hot, right out of the pan."

It looked and smelled so good it brought tears to Lovely's eyes. He thought of the flounders. Only that morning, they had been frolicking on the sandy bottom of Dorchester Bay.

"Awful nice of you, Pete, but I'll have to pass this time."

"What?!" he demanded. Have you lost your mind?"

Lovely nodded sadly. "I think so."

CHAPTER FIFTEEN

At 5:20 p.m., a black Mercedes pulled into the parking lot of the South Hills Country Club. From his parking space in the corner of the lot, Lovely watched Alessandro Vermino step out. He looked to be in his sixties, medium height and fit, with a full head of silver hair. He wore Nantucket reds and a white polo shirt.

The don strode to the clubhouse down the center of the walkway, forcing a rake-toting groundskeeper half into the hedge. Vermino emerged ten minutes later with three other men. They loaded up two carts. Lovely walked past them down the cart path. For the next three holes, he shadowed them from the trees lining the fairways. Near the fourth green, he found the opportunity he had been waiting for. Vermino had just chipped onto the green. He was alone, fifty feet from the nearest player. Lovely walked up to him.

"Excuse me, Mr. Vermino, I need to ask you a question. What do you have going with Roland Moore?"

Vermino gave him a puzzled look. "Who are you?"

"How about Allen Pierce?"

Vermino's expression grew irritable. "What is this shit?"

"Andrew Winthrop?"

Vermino turned on his heel.

"Wait," Lovely said in a low voice. "You don't want me shout my last question."

Vermino stopped. He turned slowly around.

Lovely said, "Why are you trying to kill David Kantor?"

"Hey Al," one of the golfers called. "You making deals or playing golf?"

Vermino turned to go.

"Don't make me ask again in a louder voice," Lovely said.

Vermino turned back and stared at him with such menace it made Lovely's skin crawl. "I never heard of the guy."

With his adrenalin pumping, Lovely's experience of time had slowed almost to a stop. In the resulting slow motion, he could plainly see on Vermino's face the fleeting grimace a liar makes when uttering a lie.

"Damn," Lovely heard himself observe, "you're no better at lying than anyone else."

By the time he got back to his car, with the adrenalin rush fading, he knew it hadn't been a wise thing to say.

* * * * *

There were no parking spaces on West Canton Street, so Lovely left his car on Columbus Avenue in front of a 150-year-old Gothic Revival church. In Lovely's boyhood, the South End had been a slum. Entire blocks of Victorian townhouses lay vacant, and scores were being torn down every year. On Sunday mornings, Lovely and his mother would drive through the crumbling streets to that church, where they would tutor a group of inner-city children about Lovely's age. None of the participants appeared to enjoy the process very much. When Lovely commented on this, and asked why they were doing it, his mother said, "Because they must learn to read."

"But why us?"

"Because we already know how."

In his mother, the liberal and the aristocrat coexisted without apparent tension.

Charlotte Shearson, David Kantor's downstairs neighbor, had shoulder-length blonde hair and gray eyes which looked unnaturally large through the thick lenses of her glasses. Her T-shirt bore the banner of the Boston *Progressive*, a popular weekly. Like Andrew Winthrop, Charlotte had a double parlor separated by sliding oak doors. But she had only two floors to live on, so her front parlor had to serve as both office and living room. She had set up a desk facing the bay window. When she wasn't staring at her computer screen, she could admire the Victorian ambience out on West Canton Street.

"I spoke to Jaimee this morning," Charlotte said when they were seated. "I didn't realize David had left without telling anyone where he was going. It's worrisome."

"Yes."

"I may have a lead for you. He's been spending a lot of time with his rental broker lately, and from the way they smooch and giggle in the hall, I'd venture to guess they're not discussing real estate."

"Who is she?"

"Adrienne Forest. She owns Tremont Realty, around the corner on Tremont Street."

"I'll speak to her."

"She may not be forthcoming. She wears a wedding ring, and when she and David leave the building, they always walk a yard apart."

"You're very observant."

She laughed. "Nosy, you mean. Also, I work out of this apartment, so I'm always around."

"What do you do?"

"I'm a journalist."

"For the *Progressive*?"

"Yes, I'm a member of the Boston literati. I like to think of myself as a twenty-first-century version of Oliver Wendell Holmes—you know, 'Here's to the City of Boston, the home of the bean and the cod, where Cabots speak only to Lowells, and the Lowells speak only to God.'"

Lovely smiled. "You write poetry, then?"

"Well, no, I mostly cover politics. Officially, I'm the political editor, but don't let the title impress you. The entire staff could sit comfortably around my dining room table. In fact, they'd probably be more comfortable in my dining room than in that stuffy office, with our boss, a sixty-year-old hippie, smoking clove cigarettes—and occasionally other things.

Which is why you can usually find me here."

"And I'm glad I did. Have you seen David or Adrienne Forest in the last three weeks?"

"No."

"Did anyone stop by David's apartment yesterday or last night?"

"Not that I noticed. But I was out of the house for part of the afternoon, and I go to sleep pretty early."

Lovely paused. "Since you're observant, tell me about David. I've never met him."

"I'm very fond of David. He's an inveterate glad-hander, but it's sincere. He likes people and likes to make them happy." She smiled. "He makes the occasional pass at me, even though he knows it's futile. If it were someone else, it would irritate me, but when David does it, it's endearing. He wants everyone to be in love with him."

"Why is it futile?"

She hesitated for a moment then said, "I'm a lesbian."

Lovely caught a glimpse of the decision-making process. She had judged him to be sympathetic, or at least safe.

"But that's how David is," Charlotte said. "He can't resist a challenge."

"I have a feeling you'd be a challenge for anyone, man or woman."

Charlotte laughed. "You're observant, too."

"If David were to get himself in trouble, what would be the cause?"

"His ambition or his fascination with women. He has too much of both."

So it seemed. "And what can you tell me about Jaimee?"

"She's bewitching, isn't she? You just want to take her in your arms and make that sadness go away. Don't you?"

Lovely let the question pass. "Do you think she could be up to something shady?"

After a moment's silence, Charlotte shook her head. "She's too lacking in guile."

"What about Adrienne Forest?"

"I don't know her well enough to judge."

"All right, I'll find out for myself." Lovely handed Charlotte his card. "Please call me if you see or hear anyone go into David's apartment." He rose to go then stopped. "Can I ask you a question about city politics?"

"Go ahead."

"Mayor Riordan: is he clean?"

"Oh, yes—as clean as an inflatable doll right out of the box."

Lovely smiled wryly. "Will he have any trouble getting re-elected?"

"Are you kidding? He could be mayor forever. He's articulate and telegenic—what a smile!—and he expresses such heartfelt concern for the registered voters of this city. He agrees with everyone he speaks to and stands with the majority on every issue. Best of all, he's Irish."

"That really matters, even today?"

"Of course it matters. The Irish are the biggest voting bloc in the city. In New York, the Jews vote for blacks, the blacks vote for Italians, and the Italians will support an Irishman—as long as he promises not to mess with their city contracts. But in Boston, it's every ethnic group for itself. The Irish hate the blacks, the blacks resent the Jews, the Jews resent the Yankee aristocracy, and the Cabots and the Lowells speak only to their stock brokers."

CHAPTER SIXTEEN

Lovely sat in his car, watching a pair of pigeons peck at a half-eaten cinnamon roll on the sidewalk. Jaimee lived right around the corner and he had a lot to tell her. But much of it was disturbing, and on a day like this, when his compassion felt like a sanded fingertip, speaking to her on the telephone would be less painful. There was a problem, however: his feeling of being watched had evolved into a feeling of being listened to.

Lovely opened his car door. The pigeons stopped eating and poised for flight. "Go ahead and eat," he grumbled, and climbed out the other side.

Jaimee buzzed him in and met him at the apartment door. She was dressed in blue jeans and a yellow halter top. She had left her feet bare.

"Sorry I didn't call first," Lovely said. "I'll explain."

"That's ok. I was just leaving to pick up my daughter at day care. Will this take long?"

"It might."

Her smile faded. "Is David all right?"

"As far as I know."

"I'll call day care and tell them I'll be another hour."

She made the call and offered Lovely a drink, which he declined. He wanted to get the delivery of bad news behind him as quickly as possible. He told her about the files disappearing during the night, and Winthrop apparently expecting his visit, and the prowler showing up while they were having their first meeting.

"You and I discussed all these things by phone, beforehand. Did you mention them to anyone else?"

She paused then shook her head. "I spoke to Irene

Freeman that one time when she gave me your name. The only other person I've spoken to is Roland, and that was before you told me about Andrew or the files."

"Did you tell anyone about my soft spot for cats?"

She stared at him blankly for a moment. "Oh, right, you mentioned that. No, I didn't tell anyone."

Lovely nodded. "Makes me wonder if your phone is tapped."

The color drained from her face. "Why would someone do that?"

"To hear information that would lead them to David."

"Someone's looking for him?"

"Yes. There's no gentle way to tell you this, so I'm just going to say it: I think a mobster put a contract on him."

Jaimee stared at him in stunned silence. "You mean...to kill him?"

"Yes."

"Good God." She fell back against the couch. After a moment, she said, "Why?"

"I don't know."

She lapsed into silence. Lovely watched her struggling with the unimaginable: the Mafia, which until now had existed only on her television, had just entered her life.

"Is he involved with the mob, then?"

"Not necessarily. He's apparently not a member of the organization that's after him. I'm wondering if somebody hired these mobsters. Can you think of anyone who might want David out of the way?"

"God." She paused then shook her head. "No."

"What about Allen Pierce?"

"Allen? He wouldn't do something like that!"

"He threatened me this morning." Lovely told her about the encounter.

"I'm sure that was just bluster. That's what men do when they're angry at each other."

"Marcia Paige seemed to think him capable of murder."

Jaimee waved her hand irritably. "Marcia. She overreacts to everything, and she hates Allen because she's in love with David. She's not fond of me, either, for the same reason."

"Maybe not, but she didn't suggest you were involved in David's disappearance. She was quite certain Allen was."

"I don't believe it. But I guess I could be wrong."

"Ok. I also met with Roland Moore yesterday. I don't mean to pry, but I wonder if all this could have something to do with your relationship with him."

"No," she said wearily. "It's nothing serious, and even if it were, he knows it's over between David and me. He has no reason to harm David."

"Maybe David found out about the two of you, and he and Roland had a falling out over it. Even an *ex*-husband can get jealous."

"Yes, but it wouldn't be like David to get upset about that kind of thing. By the time I picked up my last few boxes at the condo, I could tell he'd already had women spending the night. He was never one to look back."

Lovely chewed on his pencil. He couldn't shake the feeling that Roland Moore, with his lies, was up to something.

"If David were to die," he said, "what would happen to his interest in the real estate he owns with Roland?"

Something flickered across Jaimee's face.

"What?"

She hesitated, then said slowly, "David explained that to me once. They bought some special life insurance, so the heirs of the deceased would get paid off by the insurance company. That way, the surviving partner wouldn't find himself in business with a widow or an estate."

There was silence.

"So if David dies," Lovely said, "Roland gets his share of the real estate for nothing."

"Well, yes..."

"How much is David's half worth?"

"I...I don't know. A lot. At least a few million."

Lovely raised his eyebrows.

"There's no way!" she said. "Roland's not a murderer!"

"Is he in love with you?"

"No."

"Are you in love with him?"

"God, no." She sighed. "Do we have to talk about this?"

"No."

She turned and looked out the window. "You must think I'm pretty awful, having an affair with my ex-husband's partner."

"I don't." Based on past experience, Lovely expected people to make untidy decisions about love relationships.

"I don't know what it is about Roland," she said. "Well, I guess I do. He has this way of making you feel like you're the most desirable woman in the world. He's like a drug. When you're with him, you don't feel anything but him." She paused. "Part of it is the way he looks—like that prince you always dreamed of when you were little. You figure if he means half of what he says, you must be pretty special."

"Does he mean what he says?"

She laughed humorlessly. "No. Well, he thinks he means it, but he doesn't. He just likes to collect pretty things. I'm in the same category with his Isfahan Oriental carpet, his vintage Porsche, and his R.L. Moore Private Stock."

"Private Stock?"

She rolled her eyes. "He owns a part interest in a vineyard out in the Nashoba Valley, and every year, he gets a couple of cases of wine with his own pretty label on it." She shook her head. "There's another one headed for destruction. He comes across so smooth and sophisticated, but there's part of him that's incredibly naive. He tells such pretty lies, and he's convincing because he believes them. But he's spent so many years believing his own fluff, he can't tell when people are lying to him. One of these days, some sweet-talker is going to get him into serious trouble."

"A sweet-talking mobster, maybe?"

"No. Even Roland has enough sense not to get involved with the mob."

"Does David?"

She paused for a long moment. "God, I don't know. I hope so. I couldn't stand another death."

"Another?"

A sad self-mocking smile appeared on her face. "You really want to hear this?"

"Yes."

"My father was a big outdoorsman. First it was hiking, then rock-climbing, then mountaineering. He died in a snow storm a thousand feet from the summit of Mount McKinley. I was nine."

"I'm sorry."

She nodded vaguely. "Three years later, my brother crashed his dirt bike into a tree and was killed. He would never wear his helmet. My mother was always yelling at him for that. But he was a good kid. Then, when I was a junior in high school, my boyfriend died in a car accident. He was coming home from a party, a little drunk, a little stoned, having fun like he always did on the twisty road that ran by the river. Danny Rosen. He was such a sweet guy. He used to help my little sister with her algebra homework. At the funeral, she cried as much as I did." Jaimee was silent for a minute; then she shook her head. "The Yanomami think we are fools because we don't drink the ashes of our dead."

Lovely blinked. "What?"

She smiled the self-mocking smile again. "Sorry. I'm talking about the Yanomami Indians in the Venezuelan rain forest."

"Oh, the photographs on the wall."

She nodded. "They burn their dead and drink a small amount of the ashes mixed with water. That way, they know they're carrying their lost ones with them forever."

"You visited them?"

"I lived with them: three months during my junior year in college as part of an anthropology project, and another year after I graduated." Her eyes drifted to the eight-by-tens on the wall. "Their lives are so simple. They wear no clothes. They own nothing but their weapons, hammocks, and cooking pots, all of which they make themselves. They spend their days hunting and gathering, or just lying around in their hammocks watching the children play. Some anthropologists believe the

Garden of Eden is a cultural memory of our time as hunter-gatherers, and I can believe it."

"Why didn't you stay?" Lovely was thinking he never would have left.

"I would have liked to. But I don't have the skills, which they develop from childhood, to sustain myself in that environment." She paused. "This thing I have about simplicity—it was one of the conflicts I had with David. I couldn't wait to get out of that three-story condo and move into someplace small." She stopped talking and glanced at Lovely. "Why am I telling you all this?"

"Because I'm listening."

She nodded thoughtfully. Then she looked at him again, more closely. "And what about you? You know my life story, and all I know is your name and occupation. How'd you wind up as a private investigator?"

"I was a cop for twelve years, and I'd had enough."

"Why?"

"Too much ugliness. People beating each other up, robbing each other, overdosing on drugs. Violent criminals walking out of jail after serving twenty days; cops knocking them around to even the score."

"Didn't you know it would be that way?"

"Yeah, but it didn't bother me so much at first."

"I always assumed cops got inured to that kind of thing."

"Most do. Somewhere along the way, I guess I made a decision—not a conscious one—to break the barriers down instead of building them up; to notice more rather than less."

Jaimee was lying back against the couch, legs stretched out, bare ankles crossed. "You know about my love life, if you can call it that. Tell me about yours. You're wearing a ring, but it's on the wrong hand. Are you divorced? Gay? A monk?"

"Yes, no, and sometimes."

"Tell me about your marriage."

"It was a mistake," he said, using her phrase.

She laughed. "Why?"

82

"She had an opinion about everything I did and an irresistible urge to express it. The best part of the marriage was the divorce."

"Why did you marry her in the first place?"

"She and my mother had some of the same qualities, so a shrink might say I was working something out."

"Did you?"

"I must have, because I bailed out after a year and haven't been involved with a woman like that since."

She laughed. "At least you learned something. I never seem to. All the men in my life have been on the brink of disaster." She shook her head. "And here I am, having a drink and a heart-to-heart talk with a guy who carries a gun."

The phone rang. Jaimee got up and walked to the bedroom to answer it. Her back was very tan above the waistline of her jeans. She paused in the doorway, feeling for the light switch. If she ever grew tired of writing software, she could make a good living modeling blue jeans.

A minute later, she came back into the room. "It was Roland," she said, rolling her eyes. "He calls me..." She stopped short, a look of fear sweeping across her face. "God, I forgot about the phone tap." She glanced over her shoulder. "The thought that someone might be listening... It's creepy."

Lovely nodded.

"What do we do?" she asked.

"I thought I'd have my counter-surveillance expert check your phones. She has a van rigged up as a mobile electronics lab. She's expensive, though. Might run you five hundred dollars."

"That's all right."

"Ok, her name is Francine Cheyette. I'll see if she can squeeze it in tomorrow. I'll need keys."

She brought Lovely her extra set. "If someone tapped my phone, does it mean they were inside the apartment?"

"Probably, unless they were law-enforcement officials with a court order for the telephone company. Or the federal government looking for terrorists."

"God, I hate this."

"I don't blame you. Had any break-ins lately?"

"Not that I know of."

"Do you keep the sliding doors in the bedrooms locked?"

"Always, and the windows, too."

"I'll check for signs of a forced entry."

Lovely made a circuit of the apartment with Jaimee watching over his shoulder. He could find no tool marks on the doors or windows, nor any broken or cut glass. All the locks were intact.

"If someone got in," Lovely said, "they must have come through the apartment door, and that has a very good lock. Does anyone else have keys to this place?"

She started to shake her head then stopped.

"Who?"

She hesitated.

"Who has them?" he asked.

"Roland. He manages the building."

CHAPTER SEVENTEEN

A street light blinked on. Eliot glanced at the dashboard clock. 7:42 p.m. Where the hell was the Ant? He was supposed to have arrived at seven. What if Allen Pierce walked out of his office? The guy kept a loaded .32 in his desk. Eliot had no desire to tail him alone.

Eliot's cell phone rang. It was the Ant.

"Sorry I'm not there, Elton."

"It's El..." Eliot's voice trailed off.

"You say something?" the Ant growled.

"No."

"I'm at the Mass General walk-in with my girlfriend. She cut her hand and needs stitches. We'll have to tail that guy tomorrow."

"Ok. Same time, same place."

Eliot hung up. Then he remembered tomorrow was his parents' thirty-fifth anniversary dinner. He couldn't miss that to save the human race. And the next day was a Saturday... The Center Plaza door opened and Allen Pierce walked out, carrying a briefcase. *Oh, shit.* Eliot slid down in his seat. Why had Lovely given him this goddam assignment?

Instead of turning left, toward the parking garage, Pierce crossed the street toward Government Plaza. The right side of his suit coat was hanging lower than the left, the way Lovely's did when he was carrying a gun in his pocket. As Pierce walked between two parked cars, the sagging pocket bumped against a trunk lid, making an audible clunk. He was heading toward the concrete stairs that led down to Congress Street. In another thirty seconds, he would be gone. Eliot said a silent prayer and climbed out of his car.

He tailed Pierce down Congress Street from a distance

of thirty yards, walking like a flamingo so his Topsiders wouldn't scuff noisily on the concrete. Why did a real estate lawyer need to carry a gun? Was he doing business with the Vermino family? Had he been informed that a "trainee" private eye fitting Eliot's description was in league with the bodyguard who had roughed up two of Vermino's men? Eliot thought of the Ant, sitting in the brightly-lit Mass General waiting room surrounded by crying babies.

A block past Post Office Square, Pierce turned onto a side street. Eliot hurried to the corner and peered around it. He could barely make out Pierce striding through the darkness on the empty street. Half way down the block, Pierce opened a door beneath an awning and disappeared.

To Eliot's relief, he found that Pierce had entered a bar with a considerable crowd. It was called the White Horse Lounge, and it occupied most of the ground floor of a small hotel. Eliot was carded by two burly men in tuxedos then permitted to enter. An island bar of polished mahogany stood at the center of the room. White-clothed tables with candles lined the walls. Eliot spotted Pierce at the back of the room, knocking on a wooden door. The door opened and Pierce passed out of sight.

Eliot slid into an empty table near the door. The crowd looked up-scale—jackets and ties, miniskirts, silk dresses. Not surprising, here on the edge of the financial district. A waitress appeared and Eliot ordered a club soda.

One of the tuxedoed bouncers crossed the room and knocked on the door Pierce had passed through. Eliot slipped out of his chair. As the man entered the room, Eliot caught a glimpse of Pierce. He was seated across from a large desk, briefcase open, a wad of greenbacks in his hand. Eliot hurried back to his table. He had no idea what he had just witnessed, but it looked rotten.

Ten minutes later, Pierce emerged from the office. He stood still for a moment, surveying the room. His glance settled on a young woman in a sleeveless silver dress and matching hair ribbon. Her white-blonde hair was streaked with silver. She was pretty, but very young-looking—Eliot would have guessed late teens, but she had to be twenty-one to get through the door. Pierce sat beside her at the bar. He ordered a drink then turned to her and struck up a conversation.

He was very smooth. Eliot never got anywhere with women who listened, because he couldn't think of anything to say. The girl was smiling at Pierce and nodding, obviously interested. How did guys like that do it? Pierce wasn't bad looking, except for the zits on his chin, but he was no better-looking than Eliot. Confidence was everything. Eliot watched the woman. She looked a little spacey, like she might have had too many drinks. Maybe she was depressed or something. Maybe she had just broken up with her boyfriend and was out looking for someone to soothe the pain. If she only knew Pierce had a gun in his pocket and a payoff in his briefcase.

Pierce polished off a second drink and whispered something to her. They got up and walked past Eliot's table, leaving the scent of her perfume in their wake, then went out through the side door to the hotel lobby.

Eliot couldn't believe it. He abandoned his untouched club soda and hurried after them. On his way across the bar, a young woman caught his eye and smiled at him. He smiled back. Their eyes locked until he passed out of the room. The babes in this place sure were friendly.

Eliot entered the lobby and spotted Pierce and his companion boarding the elevator. There was no doubt about it: Pierce had scored in less than fifteen minutes. Eliot heard a sound behind him and turned around. It was the young woman who had smiled at him.

"Would you like to come upstairs?" she asked.

Eliot almost swallowed his tongue. For a full ten seconds he was unable to speak. Then he heard himself say, "You...you're staying here?" He wondered, vaguely, if these two were part of a group of crazy coeds on a road trip.

She gave him a puzzled look. "Staying?"

Then, at last, he understood.

"I have to go!" he croaked, and bolted out the front door.

* * * * *

Eliot was standing behind a parked van when Pierce came out of the hotel, thirty minutes later. Pierce walked briskly up the sidewalk and Eliot followed, a hundred feet back. It was past eight p.m. and the financial district was deserted. Eliot thought he saw Pierce glance over his shoulder. He fell back another fifty feet. On the far side of Post Office Square, Pierce turned a corner and disappeared from view. This section of town was a maze, and Eliot knew he was in danger of being shaken. He sprinted to the corner and looked around it. No one in sight. Eliot could see another side street half a block away. Pierce must have already reached it. Eliot hurried after him. Ten paces down the sidewalk, someone loomed out of a doorway. Eliot stopped short. Pierce stepped toward him, his hand in the right pocket of his jacket.

Eliot heard his mind shout, "Run!" but his feet wouldn't move. Pierce walked up to him, so close Eliot could smell the hooker's perfume on his clothes. The lawyer's expression was as blank as a cadaver's. Eliot could feel himself trembling.

"What do you want?" Pierce asked in a low, hard voice.

"N...nothing!"

"I saw you in the White Horse. You followed me when I left."

Eliot shook his head vehemently.

Pierce's hand came out of his coat pocket. It held a small stainless steel automatic. He pressed the side of the barrel hard against Eliot's cheek. "You're working for that private investigator. Don't lie to me."

"Not...lying," Eliot said, his voice so choked it was barely audible.

A car came out of the side street behind Pierce, lighting up Eliot's face.

"P...police," Eliot lied.

Pierce slipped the gun in his pocket and glanced over his shoulder. Eliot spun around and started to run. Pierce grabbed for him, catching the back of Eliot's windbreaker.

Eliot threw his arms out behind him. The windbreaker tore off. Eliot didn't stop running till he reached Government Center.

CHAPTER EIGHTEEN

Lovely crossed over Boston Harbor on the Tobin Bridge, heading north. Down below, the water looked as smooth and black as obsidian. A brightly-lit ferry, making the crossing from Rowe's Wharf to the airport, seemed palm-sized from that height.

Lovely agreed with Charlotte Shearson's assessment of Jaimee: she was completely without guile. Her candor was a breath of fresh air, a pleasure after the dissembling trio of Moore, Pierce, and Winthrop. But then, it would have been a pleasure anytime. Lovely knew a bit more about her sadness, now. He reminded himself that he couldn't make it go away. Or maybe he could, but it would only come back, because it was rooted in the past, not the present. Still, the yearning to try was almost irresistible. Charlotte had been right about that, too.

On the far side of the Harbor, Lovely left Route One and entered Chelsea. Two centuries earlier, it had been a rural community. Farms occupied the lowlands, and wealthy Boston families maintained summer homes atop the town's hills. By 1900, the landscape had changed beyond recognition. An industrial wasteland covered half the city—junk yards, dock yards, factories—and the rest was a dense stew of European immigrants. "If you don't behave," Boston parents would tell their children, "I'll send you to Chelsea."

In 1908, one of the junk yards caught fire and a quarter of the city burned to the ground. During the 1950's, a freeway pushed through the two-square-mile community, cutting it in half. In 1973, another junk yard caught fire, and another quarter of the city burned. In 1990, the city went bankrupt. So rife was it with political corruption, the court felt obliged to impose a new system of government. But after each calamity, Chelsea, like Freddie Wilson's cat, came back.

Lovely drove through a neighborhood of Victorian townhouses, several of which were undergoing renovation, and entered a district of handsome brick apartment blocks built on the ashes of the first fire. He pulled over in front of the Garden Cemetery. Lovely's uncle Myron had worked in a wire and cable mill on the Chelsea waterfront. He had been the leader of a group of employees trying to organize the mill-workers into a union. When Lovely was six, Myron's house was firebombed and he died in the blaze.

On the drive home from the funeral, Lovely had said to his father, "It isn't fair. Uncle Myron was just trying to help those people. Why did God let this happen?"

Mr. Lovely remained silent for a minute, as he often did before answering a question. Then he said, "Fairness isn't God's responsibility. Fairness is up to us."

Francine Cheyette, the counter-surveillance expert, lived in a rambling Victorian house half a mile from the cemetery. Lovely pulled into the driveway and parked behind her electronics van. Francine stood in the flood-lighted yard in front of a smoky charcoal grill. She had a round smiling face, salt and pepper hair, and a stout body resulting from her expertise as a chef. Lovely climbed out of his car. The smell of barbecuing chicken filled the air.

"Maxwell!" It wasn't his real name, but try to tell her that. "What a nice surprise! You're right on time for dinner." She speared a chicken breast and handed it to him on a paper plate. "You'll need a napkin," she said, pointing toward the picnic table.

Lovely gazed at the piece of chicken, coated with sauce and gently browned. Steam rose from it. He thought of the pigeons pecking at the cinnamon roll on Columbus Avenue. He couldn't do it.

He sighed. "Looks great, Francine, but I seem to be a vegetarian this week."

"Health reasons?"

"Well...sort of."

She winked at him. "Feeling sorry for the little animals, Maxwell?"

"That could be part of it, too."

Francine removed the plate from his hands. "Eat some coleslaw and potato salad instead," she instructed.

"Ok, Ma, thanks."

She laughed.

"Speaking of the maternal instinct," Lovely said as he dished out the coleslaw, "don't you worry about leaving your van in the driveway with all that expensive equipment in it?" The old one-car garage was allocated to her husband's convertible.

"I pity the thief who tangles with my van. I installed alarms on all the doors, an infrared-detector in case they climb through a window, and a motion-detector in case they try to tow it. Caspar the Friendly Ghost couldn't steal the thing. Now, what brings you to Chelsea?"

"I have a client who needs her phones checked. I'm worried some mobsters are eavesdropping on her."

Francine gave him a sharp look. "The last time we did a job like that, we got shot at."

"We didn't get hit."

"Oh, that makes me feel a whole lot better."

"It'll be ok. Her apartment is right on a busy street, and I've been in and out of it several times in the past few days. I haven't seen any mobsters lurking about."

Francine gave him a dubious look.

"Really, if I thought there was any danger, I wouldn't ask you to do it."

"Are you planning on going in with me?"

"Of course."

"Well, all right," she said without enthusiasm. "If you think it's safe."

"Can you fit me in tomorrow?"

She paused. "I could squeeze you in at lunchtime, between twelve and one."

"That'll be fine. I'll meet you in front of her building at noon." Lovely gave her the address, thanked her for the vegetarian fare, and headed back to his car.

"Maxwell," she called after him.

He turned around.

"If her phones were wired by pros, they probably bugged her apartment, too."

Lovely nodded slowly. "I hadn't thought of that. You'll have to sweep the whole place." He drove home, thinking about what he had said in Jaimee's apartment, and who might have been listening.

Lovely let himself into his apartment and dropped into his swivel chair. A piece of paper on which he had written Roland Moore's name and phone number was lying on top of the desk. Lovely wrote "lying asshole" across it and stabbed it to the desk with a box-cutter.

His eyes drifted around the room, coming to rest on the dusty sound system, a vintage Pioneer tuner and turntable, rarely used since he had come to prefer silence. The speakers were as big as steamer trunks—the quality that had recommended them to nineteen-year-old Max when he had purchased them. Lovely smiled wryly at the memory. Then his smile faded, and he shoved himself out of his chair. He had just realized what had bothered him about Mrs. Grybowski's CD player: no speakers.

Lovely grabbed a milk crate from the garage and crossed the side yard, past the yew hedge where he had found Mrs. Grybowski's body, and the maple tree that had taken two bullets intended for Lovely. Lights were on upstairs in the Sullivans' apartment, and Lovely could hear a television playing, but Mrs. Grybowski's place was silent and dark. It seemed to him to emanate finality. Soon her heirs would come and pack up her life's accumulation of possessions. Then Mr. Sullivan would repaint the apartment and rent it out to someone new.

Lovely put the crate in front of Mrs. Grybowski's bedroom window and stepped up on it. He shined his flashlight through the glass. Everything was just as he remembered it. Except for the CD player: it had vanished.

Lovely picked up the crate and headed back to his

house, following the footprints his shoes had left in the wet grass. He could surmise what had happened: The "CD player" was a receiver and voice-activated recorder installed by the prowler to monitor the bugs he had intended to plant in Lovely's apartment. It wouldn't have been difficult for the prowler to cook up a story for the gullible Mrs. Grybowski. When she saw him in the yard that night, she must have gone out to ask him what in the world he was doing prying up Mr. Lovely's screens. The prowler, guessing she would report the incident to Lovely, decided she was becoming an obstacle, and he had to get rid of her.

Sometime after the murder—perhaps the night he made the attempt on Lovely's life—the prowler had broken in and removed his equipment, so it couldn't be traced to him. Finality.

Back in Lovely's apartment, a flashing light on his telephone indicated a missed call. He listened to an hysterical voicemail from Eliot describing his encounter with Allen Pierce. Lovely had heard of the White Horse—a notorious hooker bar, which only Eliot could have mistaken for a singles club. The next message came from Ralph Henman.

"Hi, Max! Did my best to find another place for Cyrus, but nothing worked out. Brigitte and I are leaving early in the morning, so I'll bring him by tonight. Thanks again."

Lovely put his head in his hands and groaned. The doorbell rang. He plodded to the door and pushed it open. "Ralph."

Henman grinned and held up the cat. "Sure is good of you, Max!"

Cyrus meowed a greeting, showing his monstrous teeth. His bulky physique and contentedly menacing presence reminded Lovely of the Ant. Henman put him down. Cyrus glanced around, sniffing the air, then trotted off toward the kitchen.

"I'll get his things," Henman said. He returned with a melon crate.

"Cyrus gets a can of food in the morning and another in the evening. He likes to eat his evening meal when he wakes up from his nap, around five or six o'clock, so try to be home at that hour to feed him."

"I'll plan my day around it."

"He has a urinary tract condition," Henman continued, "so he can only eat this special food. No table scraps, no milk, and definitely no seafood. Now, this food has a high fat content, and the fat congeals at room temperature. So you have to heat it up a little or he won't eat it. Not so hot that it's steaming, just warm. About body temperature."

"Maybe I could put a spoonful on my wrist to test it."

"That would work." Henman withdrew a DVD from the melon crate. "Cyrus gets bored when he's left alone in the house, so we bought him this video of birds and rodents. Just leave it playing on your TV."

"I don't have a DVD player."

"Oh-oh. I guess I'll have to run home and get ours."

"That's all right," Lovely said quickly. "There's a birdfeeder outside the kitchen window. He can watch that."

"Ok. If you let Cyrus out, he'll wind up back at our house. But he needs his exercise, so we brought you this." Henman pulled a leash out of the crate. "You can take him for walks, morning and evening."

Lovely resisted the urge to twist the leash around Henman's throat.

"Now," Henman said, "about the cat box..."

When Henman was gone, Lovely placed a call to Marcia Paige and told her about the payoff Eliot had witnessed at the White Horse Lounge.

"Allen represents the owners before the city licensing authorities," she said. "They have frequent problems."

Lovely could well believe it. "Any idea why they'd be paying him in cash?"

"Probably so Allen can cheat on his taxes."

"They're not up to anything more criminal than that?"

"I wouldn't know."

Lovely thanked her and hung up. Tomorrow, he'd find out if Vermino had a hand in the White Horse Lounge.

Cyrus padded into the room.   He hopped up on Lovely's lap and took a seat facing the aquarium. Lovely felt like he had a cinderblock on his thighs. He brought in a chair from the kitchen, placed it beside the gar's tank, and put Cyrus on it.   The gar was drifting just below the surface.   Cyrus leaned forward and batted at the glass with his paw. The gar bolted away, splashing water. Cyrus sat back on his haunches. He looked pleased.

Lovely wagged his finger. "No seafood, Cyrus."

They settled in to watch.

CHAPTER NINETEEN

Lovely was startled into wakefulness by a phone ringing inches from his ear. He jumped and looked around. He had fallen asleep with his head on his desk. Cyrus, curled up in the chair, glanced at him uncertainly. Lovely checked the clock. 2:04 a.m. He picked up the phone.

"It's Charlotte Shearson," the caller said in a hoarse whisper. "Someone's upstairs in David's apartment."

"Did you see them?"

"No, I just woke up a minute ago when the front door closed. I can hear the floor creaking overhead."

"I'm on my way. Call me on my cell phone if anything changes."

Lovely picked up Soldiers Field Road and raced toward Boston. Beginning at the Harvard Business School, the parkway passed beneath a series of cross streets. At each underpass, the road dropped sharply, flattened out for a few car-lengths, then climbed steeply back to ground level. At the speed limit, forty-five, the stretch was like a roller coaster. Lovely entered it at seventy.

He sailed down the first decline and hit the flat section at the base, bottoming out his shocks with a bang and a violent scrape. There was another scrape and he was heading upward. His car left the ground at the top of the rise, landing front-wheels-first. The hood popped open. It was caught by the second latch. The car swerved then straightened out. Lovely rounded a bend and plunged into the next depression. His cell phone rang. He hit bottom, flew out of the underpass, and grabbed the phone.

"I locked the person in the building!" Charlotte whispered gleefully.

"How?"

"There's a door from my bedroom that comes out under

97

the front stoop. I slipped outside, climbed the front steps, and wrapped wire around the handles of the double doors."

"What about the back stairs?"

"When David renovated the building, he built them into my unit. You can't get to them from the hall."

"I'm not sure you should have done that, Charlotte. If the person got into the building by picking the lock, he may try to get out by picking the lock on your apartment."

Lovely heard silence on the other end of the line.

"Do you have a chain on your door?"

"No."

Lovely sailed past Boston University, its neo-Gothic towers rising above the parkway. The road straightened out. He pushed the gas pedal to the floor.

"Where are you?" he asked.

"At my desk." She caught her breath. "He's coming down the stairs!" Half a minute passed. "He's yanking on the front doors," she whispered. "He's making a lot of noise."

Lovely left the parkway at the Fenway exit. He raced along deserted Park Drive, skirting the dark expanse of the Back Bay Fens.

"The noise stopped," Charlotte whispered.

Lovely could hear his tires squealing as he rounded the bend before the bridge over the Muddy River.

Charlotte said in a barely-audible voice, "He's trying my door."

Lovely ran through a red light at sixty. He thought of hanging up and dialing 911, but he didn't want to leave her. He'd get there before the cops anyway. He flew past Symphony Hall. Up ahead, the Huntington Avenue light turned red. Lovely kept his foot on the accelerator. A taxi pulled out in front of him. Lovely stomped on the brakes. His Chrysler skidded, pitching sideways. The cabby hit the gas and shot forward, out of harm's way.

"He's trying the front doors again," Charlotte whispered.

"I'm almost there."

"I don't know what he's doing, but he's making a

98

racket."

Lovely turned the corner onto Columbus Avenue in a full-locked slide.

"Oh, God!" Charlotte said. "He broke down the door!"

"Try to get a look at him through your window."

"It's a man—tall; he's wearing gloves. He's hurrying down the sidewalk toward Tremont Street."

Lovely slowed and turned onto West Canton Street. He spotted a man fifty feet ahead on the right-hand sidewalk. It looked like the prowler. Lovely yanked his Ruger from his holster. He'd slam on the brakes, jump out, take a bead on the man over the roof of the car. *Freeze, or I'll blow you away.* Lovely was rolling to a stop. The man was twenty feet ahead, walking briskly. He glanced over his shoulder at Lovely's headlights and stopped short. Then he spun around and sprinted up the sidewalk past Lovely's car.

Lovely cursed, U-turned, ran out of room, backed up, completed the turn in time to see the man duck into a fire lane. Lovely raced down the block and entered the alley. The man was a hundred yards ahead of him, still running. Lovely screeched to a halt. A Saab idled in the fire lane. A slender leg protruded from the open passenger door. Lovely could see a couple inside saying a leisurely good night. He laid on the horn. The slender leg disappeared and the Saab pulled over. Up ahead, the running man reached the end of the fire lane and turned right, toward Columbus Avenue. Lovely inched past the chatting couple. The left side of his car scraped a pair of plastic trash cans, knocking one over. He raced to the end of the lane and turned right. The man was not in sight.

Lovely drove to the end of the block and stopped halfway out on Columbus Avenue, scanning the broad well-lit boulevard. He spotted the man ducking onto a side street. Lovely raced down Columbus and turned the corner. He stopped short. The man had left the street and was running through an adjacent park. Lovely jumped out and went after him.

The park was a rectangle the size of a city block. A small playground occupied one end and basketball courts the other. In between was an expanse of lawn relieved by shrubbery and park benches. The man was running diagonally across the lawn, following the path of a paved walkway. He was a hundred and fifty yards ahead of Lovely and moving fast, but he had to be getting winded. His car, in all likelihood, was blocks behind them on West Canton or Tremont. Lovely felt the weight of his Ruger in his hand. This time, the prowler wasn't getting away.

At the far corner of the park, the man turned onto the street that bordered it and disappeared behind a row of brick townhouses. When Lovely reached the street, he saw the man round the corner onto Huntington Avenue, heading toward Copley Place. The distance between them was shrinking. Lovely slowed as he neared Huntington, taking the corner wide in case the man might be lying in ambush. He wasn't. Lovely could see him a block down the street, climbing into a taxi in front of the Marriott Hotel. The door slammed shut and the cab raced off down the street. Lovely stood on the sidewalk panting as it drove out of sight.

Lovely retraced his steps. There was no need to rush. It would take the man two minutes to reach his car by cab. He'd be long gone before Lovely could get there.

Lovely's old Chrysler had a ticket on the windshield: fifty dollars for double-parking. He stuffed it in his pocket. He pushed down the hood, making sure it latched securely, and drove around the corner to West Canton Street. The steps leading to Charlotte's front door were littered with splintered wood. A century-old brass knob set had been torn from one of the double doors. Charlotte had wired the doors shut from the inside. Lovely rang her bell.

"Are you all right?" she shouted from the other side of the glass. She hurriedly unwrapped the wires and let him in.

"Fine, except he got away. How about you?"

"I was scared to death for a minute, but I'm ok."

Lovely gestured toward the entrance. "He made quite a mess, didn't he?"

She nodded sadly. "That door is a hundred and fifty years old. David will die when he sees it."

Her words hung in the air.

"God," she said, "I hope he's ok. I went upstairs. His apartment is locked, and everything looks normal from the hall."

"I'll take a look. And tomorrow I'll borrow Jaimee's keys and go inside." He started up the stairs.

"I'm not sure, but I think I saw that man once before."

Lovely stopped short and turned. "When?"

"A week or two ago. I was out front on the sidewalk, talking to a neighbor, and a tall, thin man walked up the steps and let himself into the building. He was wearing some kind of uniform, so I assumed he was a repairman. I didn't think anything of it at the time."

"Did you see his face?"

"No."

"What color hair?"

She paused to think. "Dark."

"Anything else you remember about the way he looked, or walked, or was dressed?"

She considered it for moment then shook her head.

"Did he have keys?"

"He must of, unless it's possible to pick a lock in a few seconds."

"Not likely. Does Roland Moore manage this building?"

"Yes."

"Does anyone else have keys?"

"Not that I know of."

Without his intending it, Lovely's mouth twisted slightly.

Charlotte's eyes widened. "You don't think Roland's involved!"

Lovely just shrugged. Tomorrow, he'd pay Moore a visit.

"I doubt the thin man will come back after all this," Lovely said. "But just to be safe, keep those doors wired shut until I figure out what's going on. If he shows up, call the police first. They'll get here faster."

After a quick inspection of David's apartment door,

Lovely bid Charlotte goodnight and went back to his car. He drove to the end of West Canton St. and turned onto Tremont. There wasn't a car or pedestrian in sight. As he passed Jaimee's building, he glanced up at the top floor. The windows were dark. He thought of Roland Moore and his keys.

Lovely drove home on the deserted parkway and wound through the empty streets of Watertown. As he pulled into his driveway, he found himself scanning the bushes beside his house. He knew, now, that the prowler was linked to David Kantor, which probably meant he was working for Vermino. That, in turn, meant Lovely was being hunted not by a lone murderer, but by an organization of professional killers.

He went inside and dropped into his swivel chair. The aquarium lights were off. Cyrus dozed on a folded blanket at the foot of the bed. Lovely leaned back and closed his eyes. He saw a fleeting image of something on fire. After a minute, he realized what it was: a dream he'd been having when Charlotte's phone call awakened him. In the dream, Chelsea was burning again. Lovely climbed into bed and tried to sleep.

CHAPTER TWENTY

The Tremont Street office of David Kantor's rental broker, Adrienne Forest, took up the ground level of what once had been a single-family townhouse. As with many buildings on the block, the first two stories of the brick facade had been removed and replaced with a storefront. The gilt letters of the firm's name, Tremont Realty, glittered on the plate glass. Lovely pushed open the door.

The office consisted of a single large space with a conference room tucked into one corner. It contained a dozen desks, most of them in use. A young man sat behind a reception counter, speaking on the telephone. He smiled weakly at Lovely and raised his index finger.

"I didn't know the ceiling leaked," the man said into the phone. "Inspect it? Well, no, I didn't climb up on the roof and look for cracks." There was a pause. "I see. Have you knocked on his door and asked him to turn down the volume? Oh. No, I don't think there's anything in the condo bylaws forbidding pet pythons..."

Lovely smiled and turned his attention to the other occupants of the office. He tried to guess which of the women would be David Kantor's sweetheart. He settled on a black-haired woman in a gray suit, seated at the back of the room. She was strikingly beautiful, but very thin, and she had a haunted look about her. Lovely guessed she rarely smiled.

The receptionist said to his caller, "But if the skull and crossbones are painted on the inside of his door, I don't see what we can do."

Lovely walked past him and sat down across from the beautiful woman in the gray suit.

"Are you Adrienne Forest?"

She nodded.

Lovely handed her his card. She looked at it and stopped breathing.

"Can we talk in the conference room?" Lovely asked.

She stood up without a word and walked into the room. Lovely followed her, closing the door behind them. They sat down at the table.

"I'm not working for your husband," he said.

The tension in her face and shoulders eased.

"Don't ask me how I know, because I can't tell you. In any case, I'm not investigating your relationship with David Kantor. I was hired to find him. His wife hasn't heard from him in three weeks. Have you?"

She paused, collecting herself. "I can't answer that question."

Lovely nodded thoughtfully. "Did David tell you someone is trying to kill him?"

The color drained from her face. "What are you talking about?"

"Someone took a shot at him right before he left town."

"Oh my God." She closed her eyes and sank back against the chair. After a minute, her eyes opened and fixed on the wall above Lovely's head. Her right hand, palm-down on the table, was trembling.

"When did you hear from him last?" Lovely asked gently.

She fumbled with the clasp of her purse, took out a pack of Virginia Slims, stuck one in her mouth. She struck a match which failed to ignite, tried a second time, and a third. She threw the match into a stainless-steel ashtray and tore off another.

"Want me to light that for you?" Lovely offered.

"No!"

She finally got the cigarette lit and took a few deep drags, filling the close air of the conference room with smoke. She showed no intention of answering Lovely's question.

"I'm trying to help him, Ms. Forest. Anything you tell me will be kept in confidence."

Her eyes turned to Lovely's face. He could see the struggle between her loyalty to David and her fear for him.

"We're on the same side," Lovely said. "I was hired to keep him from getting hurt."

She sighed. "All right. I saw him the middle of last week. He told me everything was fine, he just needed to get away for a while. It's the same thing he said the day he left. I didn't believe him, but we only had a little time together and I didn't want to spoil it. I had no idea someone had tried to...hurt him. God."

"Is he having financial problems?"

"I don't think so."

"Has he ever had any dealings with loan sharks or mobsters?"

"Not that I know of."

"Was he acting unusual in the weeks before he left? Worried? Upset?"

"No."

She seemed distracted, as if Lovely's questions were beside the point. Maybe she was still recovering from the shock of what he had told her.

"Would David confide in you if he were in trouble?" Lovely asked.

"I guess so, but he's not really the type to talk about things like that. He's always in a good mood—upbeat, enthusiastic. That's the kind of person he is." She smiled a little at the thought.

"I guess his good humor is contagious."

"Yes, he cheers me up. He makes me laugh." Her smile lingered for a moment then faded.

"Sorry I had to bring you bad news," Lovely said. "Do you know where he's staying?"

She shook her head. "He wouldn't tell me. He just said he'd call again soon."

She still seemed distracted. What ruminations were taking place behind those anxious eyes?

"So," Lovely said, "what does it all mean to you?"

"I have no idea," she said. But she said it too quickly.

Lovely watched her for a moment. Then he said, pointedly, "Adrienne, do you know what trouble David has gotten himself into?"

"No!"

Lovely felt the twinge of discomfort in his gut that signaled deceit. Now he understood why his earlier questions had appeared irrelevant to her.

"You're not telling me the truth."

"I am!"

"Listen, the people who are after him are going to keep trying. They're professionals."

Her face paled again. "What do you mean?"

"Mobsters."

"Jesus, God." She put her hand on her chest.

"If I can find out what's happening, I may be able to help him. How did he get mixed up with the mob? Tell me what you know."

"I don't know *anything*." It sounded like a plea.

"I think you do."

"I told you, I *don't*." Her eyes filled up with tears.

"I'm sorry to upset you, but I need to find out what's going on."

"I have to get back to work." She mashed out her cigarette and stood up.

Lovely rose to his feet. "I'll be in touch. Call me if you change your mind."

She walked out of the conference room without saying goodbye.

CHAPTER TWENTY-ONE

The Stone Street police station took up most of a city block. A row of white columns with a triangular pediment graced the entrance of the century-old structure. The intent of the Greek-temple motif, presumably, was to give the building an air of authority. Never mind that the Greek gods were capricious and corrupt. Lovely had always thought that for a police station, the facade of the Temple of Solomon would have been more appropriate. Or at least would have set a better example.

Lovely passed through the shallow portico and went inside. The desk sergeant, a fair-haired man in his early fifties, caught sight of him and broke into a grin. "Rabbi!"

Lovely shook his hand. "Good to see you, McGann. I swear, you don't look a day older."

"That's because I'm sitting down. You look pretty fit, yourself, but I see some gray coming in."

"Yeah, must be from working so hard."

McGann snorted. "What brings you here?"

"I need to talk to Nathan Thomas."

"*Lieutenant* Nathan Thomas, you mean."

"Yeah, I knew about that."

"I'll ask if he'll grant you an audience," McGann said with a wink. He spoke briefly on the phone and sent Lovely upstairs.

Thomas's office, a small room in need of paint, had a single window too high to see out of without standing on a chair. A tepid breeze wafted out of an air-conditioning vent in the ceiling. Smiling his characteristic little smile, Thomas shook Lovely's hand and seated him across from the desk. He had a handsome, youthful face and a circle of chocolate-brown scalp showing at the top of his head.

Lovely had wondered, from time to time, what it was like for Thomas, being a black officer on an Irish-dominated police force. Lovely had been something of an anomaly himself in his day—as evidenced by the old nickname with which McGann had greeted him—so he had some idea of Thomas's situation. Lovely hadn't experienced any overt hostility. You're a cop first at Stone Street, and an ethnic oddity second. If you do your job well, you earn a measure of respect. But you're still an outsider. Thomas had never spoken to Lovely of these things—perhaps he never spoke of them to anyone—but he always seemed to enjoy having Lovely in his office.

"Have you been sleeping on a park bench," Thomas asked, "or is your iron out of order?"

Lovely glanced down at his clothes. "I made the mistake of screwing up Alessandro Vermino's golf game yesterday, and I've been a little distracted."

Thomas laughed. Then he stopped abruptly. "My God, you're not joking."

"No."

Thomas shook his head. "Doesn't sound smart, Max."

"Probably wasn't."

"Does it have to do with that lawyer you had me run through the NCIC computer the other day?"

"Yeah, I think Vermino's after him. I need to know if Vermino has any connection to the White Horse Lounge."

"I've never heard the place was mobbed up, but I'll check."

"Thanks. Also, I chased a man through the South End last night who may work for Vermino. I lost him when he got into a taxi in front of the Marriott Hotel on Huntington Avenue. That was around two-thirty a.m. I couldn't make out the cab company, but I'm sure there weren't too many fares picked up at the Marriott at that hour. I need to know where they dropped the guy off."

"The cab company won't have a record of a pick-up off the street," Thomas said, "so it'll be a matter of tracking down

108

the driver and hoping he remembers where the fare ended. I'll call you if I have any luck. More importantly, what are you going to do about Vermino?"

"I don't know. Avoid him."

"And when he comes looking for you?"

Lovely grimaced, shrugged.

"I'd ask our patrols to keep an eye on your house," Thomas said, "but Watertown's too far out of our jurisdiction. Why not hire a couple of off-duty blues to keep you company? You could bill it to the client."

"And tell her she's paying a $1000 a day because of my stupidity?" Lovely shook his head. "I don't want her worrying about this; she has enough on her mind. Anyway, Vermino won't bother with me—I'm not worth the trouble."

Thomas did not look convinced.

* * * * *

Lovely paused outside the police station and glanced at his watch. Just past ten. He wasn't due to meet Francine Cheyette until noon—plenty of time to drive home. He fiddled with his car keys, thinking about Vermino. Home was beginning to feel like an unsafe place. He decided to wait and see what turned up in Jaimee's apartment.

Lovely bought a hot pretzel from a street vendor and headed across town on foot. Twenty minutes later he reached the Esplanade, a long, narrow park on the south bank of the Charles River. He sat down on the grass, facing the water. A pair of ducks paddled in the shallows a few yards away. Farther out, an eight-man shell skimmed upstream toward the MIT boathouse. Seeing the Charles without rowers was like seeing a statue of Paul Revere without his three-cornered hat. The ducks paddled up to Lovely. He tossed them the pieces of pretzel he had saved and closed his eyes.

At first, he felt nothing but the rise and fall of his chest. The excited quacking died down, and he could hear cars passing on Storrow Drive. After a minute, he became aware of a tightness in his gut. It was subtle, but persistent. It had been there, he realized, since the day before. The muscles in his arms felt tense. He heard rapid footsteps and glanced over his shoulder. A woman in black Spandex trotted along the footpath. Lovely closed his eyes again and breathed. Every time the wind rustled the maples, it sounded like stealthy footsteps behind him. He turned around, putting his back to the river. Sometimes the tightness in his belly was a warning—a signal to do something. Other times it was simply a feeling that had to be accepted. Lovely listened to the murmur of the river and breathed into the chill inside him.

CHAPTER TWENTY-TWO

Back on Tremont Street at noon, Lovely hunkered on the stoop in front of Jaimee Kantor's townhouse. Francine Cheyette arrived ten minutes late in her husband's convertible. She climbed out of the car, glancing around, a piece of electronic equipment under her arm.

"Where's your van?" Lovely asked.

"Let's go inside."

Francine sat down on the stairs in the entrance hall and looked up at Lovely grimly.

"What's the matter?" he asked.

"My van caught fire in the driveway last night. There's nothing left but ashes and melted steel."

"My God, what happened?"

"The fire department believes an accelerant was used."

A cold feeling spread through Lovely's body. "Arson."

She nodded.

Lovely was silent for a moment. Reluctantly, he met her eyes. "The only person I told about our sweep was the woman who lives here. But I told her in the apartment. If it's wired..." He winced. "I told her about your van, too."

"I thought this job might have something to do with it. I can't think of anyone else who'd have a motive."

Lovely closed his eyes and shook his head. "I can't tell you how sorry I am, Francine. It never occurred to me something like this might happen."

She sighed. "I know, Maxwell."

"It took real courage for you to show up here. Are you still going to be able to sweep the place with all your equipment burned up?"

"Sort of. I brought this wide-band receiver into the house last night to charge the battery." She held up what looked like a portable radio. "It picks up radio transmissions across a broad band of frequencies simultaneously. The most common kind of bug is a radio frequency bug—we call it an RF. If the eavesdroppers are using one, this will find it. There are other kinds of bugs—sophisticated ones—it can't detect, but it'll have to do for now."

They started in the living room. Francine switched on her wide-band receiver and motioned Lovely to stand beside her.

"Watch the meter," she whispered.

She pointed the antenna at the wall and began moving it up and down. Then she circled the room, continuing the sweeping motion. Lovely followed, eyes on the receiver's LCD read-out. It was barely registering. Halfway around the room, the meter began to jump. Francine moved the antennae up and down, then left to right. The meter reading peaked when the antenna was pointed at an electrical outlet. She looked at Lovely and nodded grimly. She completed her circuit of the walls then checked the ceiling and floor. Radio frequency transmissions were not coming from any other part of the room.

Francine found the circuit breaker in the hall closet and switched off the apartment's electricity. Using a screwdriver, she removed the electrical outlet from the wall. She waved Lovely over and pointed. Behind the wallboard, he could see an inch-long cylindrical object wired to the electrical outlet and taped into place. Francine disconnected the wires, removed the object, and showed it to Lovely.

"It's an RF transmitter with a built-in mic," she whispered. "Rigged to leech power from the building wiring so it doesn't need batteries. This," she said, indicating a hair-thin wire coming out of the end of it, "is an antenna."

"Can anyone buy one?"

Francine shook her head. "This kind can only be sold to law enforcement agencies. But there's a black market."

Francine pointed to a tiny hole in the wall beside the electrical outlet, so small, Lovely hadn't noticed it. "That pinhole lets the sound waves through the wallboard," she whispered. "That's all it takes." She stood up. "Let's check the rest of the house."

"Wait a minute," Lovely said. He hurried into the kitchen and rummaged through the cabinets until he found a plastic bag. He brought it back to the living room. Using a handkerchief, he took the bug from Francine and dropped it into the bag.

"There won't be any fingerprints," Francine said. "Whoever did this was a pro."

Using the same method, Francine found a second bug behind an electrical outlet in the master bedroom. The other rooms were clean.

"Now for the telephones," she whispered. "If there's an RF tap on a phone, it probably won't transmit unless someone's on the line. Make a call and I'll sweep."

Lovely dialed the weather: mostly sunny, high of seventy-six, ten percent chance of rain. Francine found an RF transmitter in each telephone.

"Can we talk now?" Lovely whispered.

"Better not." Francine motioned him toward the door. They stepped out into the hall. "Like I said, there could still be bugs. This receiver won't detect burst transmissions, or a carrier current transmitter. I'll have to bring in a spectrum analyzer to be sure, and mine's in ashes. It'll take me at least a week to replace it. In the meantime, tell your client to watch what she says."

"What's the maximum range of those transmitters?"

"A thousand feet, and five hundred is more like it. For a few days, the eavesdroppers could put a receiver and a voice-activated tape recorder in the trunk of a car. But if it's been going on for weeks, like you think, they probably rented an apartment on the block. It'd be easy to find a rental in this neighborhood."

Lovely nodded. "Any way to trace the location of the receiver?"

"No. Receivers don't put out signals. How do you figure they got in to wire the place?"

"I'm guessing someone gave them keys. No signs of a

forced entry."

"Tell your client to change her locks."

Lovely sat in his car, trying to absorb the latest round of shocks. Vermino's men must have firebombed Francine's van to prevent the sweep. Counter-surveillance experts were hard to come by, so it would have bought them a week, if Francine hadn't taken the wide-band receiver into her house. Lovely glanced up at the buildings lining Tremont Street, thinking about the short range of the transmitters. The windows peered down at him like a thousand eyes. When the prowler had left David's building the night before, he had headed toward Tremont Street. Maybe he was walking home, rather than to his car as Lovely had assumed. Maybe he had planted bugs in David's apartment on the day Charlotte had first seen him, and his midnight visit had been to repair a malfunctioning device. How convenient to have both surveillance targets so close— and to have keys. Lovely started his engine. Time to pay a visit to Roland Moore.

CHAPTER TWENTY-THREE

The receptionist at R. L. Moore Design wore a sky-blue silk dress, a white chiffon scarf, and silver slippers. She looked as if she might take to the air at any moment and disappear into the simulated heavens above her desk. Her face lit up when Lovely walked through the door.

"Here to see Roland?"

"Yeah," Lovely said without enthusiasm.

She looked hurt.

"Sorry," Lovely said, forcing a smile. "It's not you—I'm just in a crummy mood."

"Well, you don't have to smile, you know."

He laughed. "Thanks for keeping me honest."

She announced his arrival and sent him back to Moore's office. Moore was lounging on the sofa.

"I just came from Jaimee's apartment," Lovely said. "You won't believe what I found."

Moore summoned up his expression of concern. Did he and Winthrop practice it together in front of the mirror?

"What?"

Lovely reached into his pocket and pulled out the plastic bag of RF transmitters.

Moore swallowed convulsively. "W...what are they?"

"Electronic eavesdropping devices."

"And...they were in Jaimee's apartment?"

"That's right, cleverly hidden in the phones and behind the walls. Isn't that shocking? I've been wondering—a lot—how they got there. Whoever installed them had keys. That's why I came to you."

"I don't know anything about it!"

"Sure you do. You gave the keys to a tall, thin man.

He's the other person who's looking for David—the one you wouldn't tell me about the other day."

Moore looked like he was about to choke. "I didn't give her keys to anyone! David has keys, too—he must be spying on her."

Lovely shook his head sadly. "You're a piss-poor liar, Roland."

Moore's expression hardened. "I don't have to listen to this crap."

"Sure you do—unless you think you can throw me out." Lovely gave him a moment to consider his chances. "Help me with this question, Roland: if David dies, what happens to his share of the property?"

Moore cocked his head. Then his eyes opened wide. "My God! You don't think... What are you saying?!"

"I'm saying if David dies, insurance pays off his heirs and leaves you with his share of the property. Isn't that true?"

"Yes," Moore sputtered. "But I wouldn't... For God's sake, you must be crazy!"

"Then why did you give that mobster the keys?"

"What mobster?!"

Lovely tapped the bag of RF bugs thoughtfully against his palm. Moore's surprise at the reference to a mobster seemed genuine. "Did you know these can't be bought in stores, Roland?" he asked, holding up the bugs.

Moore looked utterly confused. "Huh?"

"They're available only to official law enforcement agencies. But they can be obtained, via a black market, by professional criminals. That's how your tall, thin man got a hold of them."

Moore paled. For a long moment, he was silent. Then he shook his head with great determination. "I don't know anything about those things. I never gave anyone keys. And I have no idea what you're talking about."

Lovely sighed. "Roland, you're in way over your head. If you have one speck of common sense, you'll tell me about that thin man now, before you drown."

Roland was still shaking his head. "I don't know any

tall, thin man. I don't know anything about this."

Lovely tossed his business card on the coffee table and rose to his feet. "If you come to your senses, call me." He turned to go then stopped. "I almost forgot to bring this up: did you know your mobster's employers are trying to kill David?"

Roland's jaw dropped. "What are you talking about?!"

"They took a shot at him right before he left town—put a hole in his car but missed him. That's why he hasn't come back."

Roland's mouth was still open. Lovely could hear the hum of the ventilation system in the ceiling.

"Don't forget to breathe, Roland."

Moore started shaking his head again. "This is crazy." He appeared to be trying to convince himself as much as Lovely. "I think you're making it up."

"I wish I was, Roland. Believe me, I do."

CHAPTER TWENTY-FOUR

Lovely paused outside the entrance of Tremont Realty, looking through the glass door. He didn't want Adrienne Forest to duck into a restroom or slip out the back. She was speaking on the phone. When she hung up, Lovely went in. She glanced up at him and shrank back against her chair. He sat down across from her. Her lips were pressed tightly together and her hands were clenched at her sides.

"I need to speak to you in the conference room," Lovely said quietly.

She shook her head.

Lovely leaned back in his chair, listening to the buzz of voices in the office. The desks were just a few feet apart. He took out his pad and wrote,

These are electronic eavesdropping devices. They were installed in Jaimee Kantor's apartment by the people who are looking for David. Her phones were tapped, and yours may be, too. The next time David calls and tells you to meet him somewhere, he may be dead when you arrive. I'm trying to save his life. If you will tell me what trouble he's in, I may be able to help.

Lovely held up the bag of transmitters, then laid the note on the desk in front of Adrienne. Reluctantly, she read. When she finished, she stood up, stuffed the note in her pocket, and walked to the conference room. Lovely followed her in. The air smelled of stale cigarette smoke. They sat down at the table. Adrienne looked like she had just run the Boston marathon on two hours sleep.

"My husband, Marshall," she said quietly. "I've had the feeling for a while that he knows about David and me. And

118

he's an insanely jealous man."

"Jealous enough to attempt murder?"

She hesitated. "I guess I think so."

"Has he ever had any dealings with mobsters?"

"I believe so. I remember him saying, once, that he had a friend who could `take care of anything or anybody.' I didn't ask who it was."

"Any guesses?"

She thought about it then shook her head. Lovely could detect no hesitation or lack of candor.

"Does your husband know David?"

"Sure, they were classmates at Harvard Law. I met David through Marshall."

"I believe the person who planted the bugs had keys to Jaimee's apartment and David's condo. Would Marshall have been able to get them through your office?"

She shook her head. "I don't have keys to Jaimee's place."

"Any idea how he might have obtained them?"

She considered the question. "Roland Moore manages both buildings. My husband probably knows that—or would have been able to figure it out. Roland designed an addition to our house last year, and he and Marshall became friendly."

"But Roland wouldn't hand out keys to anyone."

"No, but Marshall could have come up with a pretext. He's very clever—and Roland isn't."

Lovely nodded. A consensus was building around that point. "Are you certain your husband knows about you and David?"

"No. He hasn't said anything to me about it—he has too much pride for that—but I think he suspects."

"Why?"

She sighed. "I catch him looking at me in strange ways. He asks too many questions about my schedule—as if he's trying to account for every hour. He seems angry, but he doesn't say why."

"It sounds frightening."

"It is, and it's getting worse. He's suddenly taken an

interest in balancing our checkbook—probably to see where I'm spending my money. When I'm on the phone, he appears in the room and pretends to do something so he can listen. When he..." She broke off, glancing at Lovely. She looked away and said, "When he kisses me, I feel like he's watching me, and when we make love, I feel like he's testing me." She shook her head quickly, as if to throw off the memory.

"Why don't you leave him?" Lovely asked.

"I love him."

"And David?"

"I love him, too." She closed her eyes and sighed. "Every solution seems like a nightmare. I don't know how much longer I can take it." Her eyes snapped open. "You have to do something! You can't let Marshall...hurt David!"

"Are you prepared to tell your husband the truth?"

"God, I don't know what he'd do."

"Would he harm you?"

She hesitated. "I don't think so. But he'd be very angry."

"Think it over. But don't do anything without talking to me. We need some evidence your husband is connected to these mobsters and hired them. Right now, it's just speculation." He wrote his cell phone number on the back of his business card. "If you think of anything else that might be relevant, call me."

Lovely sat in his car outside Adrienne's office, watching the passing parade of South End pedestrians. A teenaged Latino couple went past, so entwined they were having difficulty walking. They were followed by two men, thirtyish, with matching moustaches. The men didn't have their arms around each other—even in the South End, there was too much intolerance for that—but they were walking close together and talking with a relaxed intimacy that made them seem like a couple. Lovely decided he couldn't blame Adrienne for falling in love with a man who made her laugh—she was badly in need of levity. But by following that impulse, she had made her life even more grim, even more frightening, than before. People had a way of doing that. In attempting to run away from the feelings haunting them, they created situations that brought the feelings upon them more intensely. Jaimee was doing it, too: involving herself with men like David and Roland who could provide some relief from her pain, only to discover that in the end, they made the pain worse. David was doing it too, no doubt, but Lovely didn't know yet what David was running from, or running to.

Lovely's thoughts turned to Marshall Forest. Another Harvard Law classmate. That made four, including David, Andrew Winthrop, and Mayor Riordan. They were turning up everywhere, like night crawlers on a rainy morning. Had Marshall made *Law Review*, too, like the other three? And what did it mean, exactly, to "make *Law Review*?" Lovely pondered the question, then dialed directory assistance. He asked for the number of the *Harvard Law Review* and placed the call.

A young woman answered with the name of the journal.

"Did you make *Law Review*?" Lovely asked.

She laughed. "Yes."

"What does it mean?"

"It means I was appointed to serve on the journal. It's a student-edited publication."

"What do you have to do to get appointed?"

"You have to get very good grades, and/or compete successfully in a writing competition."

"How many students are appointed each year?"

"This year it was forty-three."

"And you forty-three work together on the journal?"

"Right, along with the group appointed last year."

"That's a big staff."

"There's a lot of work to do. Legal scholars and practitioners from all over the country submit articles."

"Can you tell me the names of the students who were appointed from the class of 1994?"

"Hang on a minute."

She came back on the line and read through the list.

Sure enough, Marshall Forest had made *Law Review* like the other three.

It was the final name on the list, though, which jolted Lovely out of his seat: Jeffrey Zimmer—the son and law partner of Aaron Zimmer, who had represented the Verminos for as long as anyone could remember.

CHAPTER TWENTY-FIVE

Lovely hung up the phone and stared at the blank display. He had his link between Marshall Forest and the mob. He wasn't eager to break the news to Adrienne.

The phone in his hand rang, startling him out of his thoughts.

"Hello?"

"It's Adrienne. I thought of something."

"Go ahead."

"Not on the phone," she whispered.

"I'm parked out front."

Adrienne came out of her office and hurried across the sidewalk to Lovely's car. She glanced over her shoulder as she climbed in.

"Would you mind driving somewhere? I'm paranoid about my husband seeing me. His office is a mile away in the financial district, but still..."

"Of course."

Lovely drove a few blocks down Tremont and turned the corner. The side street divided into two crescent-shaped arms, which enfolded a small park. At the far end of the park, the arms merged again into a single street. Two crescent-shaped rows of townhouses enclosed the little neighborhood. The South End had a number of these small English squares. This one was called Union Park. Very Victorian and very private. Lovely pulled over and turned off his engine.

Adrienne took out her pack of Virginia Slims. "Do you want me to get out?"

"Just open the window."

She tapped out a cigarette. "It's a terrible habit and I'm trying to quit." It sounded like a well-practiced phrase.

She sat in silence, cigarette arm dangling out of the car, smoking and staring through the windshield.

"You can't tell anyone I told you this," she said. "Not ever."

"I won't."

She glanced at Lovely, then away. A pair of mourning doves were perched on the wrought-iron fence surrounding the park, throats puffing as they made their cooing call. A police car sped past, scattering the doves. Adrienne sank back in her seat.

"When my husband was a third-year at Harvard Law, he and four classmates made a pact to help each other succeed. They had all made *Law Review*, and they were—they are—five of the brightest, most talented people in the world. They called themselves the Chosen Few.

"One of the five was Keith Riordan, who's now the mayor. Even then, everyone knew he would be a great politician. The plan was to get him elected mayor, then governor, and possibly even president. Once Keith was in office, the others would get perks—lucrative city or state contracts, judgeships, cabinet appointments, maybe even a pardon now and then for a very important client. In addition to David, Marshall, and Keith, the group includes a wealthy man named Andrew Winthrop, and a lawyer named Jeffrey Zimmer. They swore an oath not to tell anyone about their group, not even wives. But Marshall told me—he tells me everything." Her voice trailed off and she looked away.

"He wouldn't tell you everything if he were having an affair," Lovely said.

"He wouldn't have an affair." She took a drag off her cigarette and blew the smoke out the window.

"How much can the others really do to help Riordan get elected?" Lovely asked. "Campaign contributions are limited to a couple thousand dollars, aren't they?"

"Yes, but there's no limit to how much you can raise for a candidate. They all hold fundraisers. And they belong to influential civic and professional groups. David, for example, joined the Chamber of Commerce ten years ago. By the time

Keith ran for mayor, David was president of the group and able to deliver an endorsement. My husband does legal work for several big unions, including the municipal employees, the teachers, and the nurses. They all endorsed Keith for his run. And Marshall's father is Benjamin Forest."

"The famous political consultant?"

"Yes. He's advised Keith on his political career, behind the scenes, from the start."

Lovely nodded. "They'd have to keep their pact a secret because it sounds so conspiratorial—it would look bad for Riordan if word got out."

"Right. Also, I think Andrew funnels cash to Keith under the table."

"Do they have regular meetings?"

"No. They limit their contacts so no one will suspect they're anything but old classmates, casual friends."

"Andrew lends money to David for his business," Lovely said.

"I know. He does the same for the others. Since he's helping them get rich, they've agreed to give him the first judgeship, and the first state supreme court appointment. Andrew wants to be a supreme court justice more than anything."

Lovely shook his head. The Chosen Few, singled out for divine favor. He didn't know whether to laugh or be horrified. He thought about it and decided to be horrified.

"Is Roland Moore involved?"

"No. I'm sure he doesn't even know the group exists."

"How about Allen Pierce?"

"No."

"He threatened me when I pushed him about David's absence. He carries a gun."

"I'm not surprised. Allen's an angry, frustrated man, and a bully. But I don't think he's dangerous."

"I understand why the group needs Riordan, Andrew, and your husband. But why David?"

"It was his idea. He was friends with the other four, and he brought them all together. He's the leader."

"The cantor," Lovely suggested.

She smiled sardonically. "Yes, the cantor."

"He leads the singing in praise of God."

"The one I'm not sure about is Jeffrey Zimmer," Adrienne said. "I've never met him, and I don't know why he was chosen."

"He and his father represent a Mafia don named Alessandro Vermino. David must have enlisted Zimmer in case the group ever needed protection, or an untraceable source of cash, or the ability to threaten someone. If you're trying to get to the top in a hurry and you're not worried about obeying the rules, a mob connection would come in handy. Winthrop could afford to pay Vermino for any services the group needed, and in any case, it would be in Vermino's interest to have a politician in office who owed him favors. It's a clever scheme." Lovely shook his head. "And now David's mobsters are after *him*." After a moment, he said, "Maybe David's disappearance doesn't have to do with Marshall after all. Maybe he had a falling out with the group."

Adrienne nodded slowly. "Or maybe he tried to quit. I remember Marshall saying it was a pact for life." She paused. "I hope Marshall doesn't know about David and me, but either way, David's in a lot of trouble. What are you going to do?"

"Speak to Roland Moore again, for starters. I think he gave Jaimee's keys to one of Vermino's men. He may have some useful information for us—if I can get him to talk."

"Will you tell me what you find out?"

"Of course."

Lovely dropped off Adrienne at her office and parked. He glanced up at the buildings lining Tremont Street, wondering if the prowler was nearby. Sooner or later he'd try for Lovely again.

Lovely leaned back in his seat and turned his thoughts to the Chosen Few. They had their law degrees and their awe-inspiring resumes, and they wanted to be rich. Except Winthrop. He was already rich, so he wanted to be on the supreme court. It reminded Lovely of a storybook he'd read as a child: the lizard dreamed of being a bird, the bird dreamed

126

of being a fish, the fish dreamed of being a lizard. The only difference was that the Chosen Few were trying to make their dreams come true—determined to do so, even if it meant getting involved with mobsters. A bunch of smart guys being very stupid.

Lovely watched a pigeon pecking at a crack in the sidewalk. He thought of the papers he had blown off Allen Pierce's conference table. It must have taken Pierce hours to put everything back in order, and as it turned out, he bore no responsibility for David's flight. Lovely felt like he'd kicked a dog. He sat there for a few minutes, cursing silently and procrastinating. Then he picked up the phone and called Pierce and Kantor, Attorneys at Law. Marcia Paige answered the phone.

"I'd like to speak to Allen Pierce, please. It's Max Lovely."

After a moment's hesitation, Marcia said, "Please hold." She came back on the line. "I'm afraid Mr. Pierce is tied up."

"Can you give him a message?"

"Yes."

"Please tell him I'm very sorry about scattering his paperwork."

"One moment." Lovely was on hold for several minutes before Marcia picked up again. "I gave him your message," she said.

"I gather his reply was lengthy, and that I don't want to hear it."

"Correct."

CHAPTER TWENTY-SIX

The receptionist at R. L. Moore Design didn't smile when Lovely walked through the door.

"You upset Roland," she said reproachfully.

"I know. I feel bad about that."

"He's been staring out the window and he's not taking calls."

"Please tell him I came to apologize and explain."

She relayed the message and sent Lovely back to Moore's office. Moore was leaning against the wall, arms folded. He looked shaken and resentful.

"I owe you an apology," Lovely said. "I thought you had something to do with David's absence, and that you hired the tall, thin man who bugged Jaimee's apartment. I was wrong. One of David's law school classmates hired the man and asked you to give him keys. I'm guessing it was Andrew Winthrop. He would have explained, plausibly, that he was worried about David's absence because of all the money you and David owe him. If you resisted giving him the keys, he probably threatened to call in your loans. You didn't know the thin man was a mobster until I told you. What I now believe is that he works for a Mafia boss named Alessandro Vermino. I believe Winthrop and three others have contracted with Vermino to have David killed."

Moore stared at him in silence for a minute. Then he shook his head slowly. "Jesus, you're not making this up."

"No."

"I had no idea Andrew was up to anything illegal. He told me he was worried David might be in trouble, and he wanted to bug the condo and Jaimee's place to find out what was going on. He said since I owned the building, I could do it legally, like they do in Manhattan to catch rent-control cheaters, and he's a lawyer. I didn't like it, but he said he had the right to call the loans if any of the signatories moved out of town. The implication was he'd foreclose if I didn't cooperate. So I gave the thin man the keys. I even told him when Jaimee comes and goes."

"What's his name?"

"Peter..." Moore's voice trailed off. "God, I don't even remember his last name."

"Don't worry, it would have been fake, anyway. Did he give you a phone number?"

"No, and I didn't think to ask for one because he was working for Andrew. I had no idea Andrew was trying to kill David!"

"I know."

Moore nodded. Then his eyes widened. "Jesus! Don't tell Andrew I spoke to you!"

"I won't."

"I called him after you left and told him what you said—about the gadgets being illegal, and Peter being a criminal. Maybe I shouldn't have done that." Moore shook his head. "God, how did I get mixed up in this?"

By worshipping the same idol as the Chosen Few, Lovely thought, but hadn't the heart to voice it.

"What did Winthrop say when you called?"

"That it was all nonsense—you're just stirring up trouble to charge Jaimee more fees. I told him what you said about someone trying to shoot David. He said that was probably a lie, too, or you'd have gone to the police. Why haven't you?"

"Because I don't know yet what illegal things David may have done, and I'm working for Jaimee."

Moore shook his head again. "I can't believe this is happening. Why would Andrew want to kill David?"

"I don't know."

Moore was silent, staring at his hand-knotted Oriental carpet. Then he looked up with a start. "What about Jaimee? Is she in danger, too?"

"I don't think so."

"Does she know about this?"

"Only that someone's after David."

He nodded. "What should I do?"

"Tell me about the thin man. What did he look like?"

Moore considered the question. "He had dark hair, cut short—almost a crew cut—and bushy eyebrows." He closed his eyes for a moment. "A prominent nose, I think. I don't remember much else."

"What was he wearing?"

Moore paused. "Some kind of uniform—like a repairman. Khaki, I think. He was only in my office for a minute."

"Did he bring back the keys?"

"At the end of the day."

"Plenty of time to copy them," Lovely noted. "He went back into David's apartment last night."

Moore shook his head grimly. "I'll have the locks changed. Jaimee's, too."

"Tell me about David's arrangement with Winthrop. What's the advantage of borrowing from him instead of a bank?"

"Lower interest rates and more leverage."

"What's leverage?"

"Andrew lets us borrow with less money down, so we've been able to buy two or three times as much real estate with the same amount of cash."

"Where does your profit come from?"

"Appreciation. Real estate values in the neighborhood have doubled in the last ten years."

"So you've doubled your money?"

"Much more than doubled it. If you buy a three-hundred-thousand-dollar building with ten percent down, and the value of the building doubles, your equity—your cash—has grown from thirty thousand dollars to three hundred and thirty thousand dollars."

Lovely whistled.

Moore nodded. "Andrew made it possible. If it weren't

for him, we'd still be small-time." There was silence for a moment. Moore glanced at Lovely, then away, a pained expression on his face. "You're thinking we'd have been better off without him."

"Yeah," Lovely said. "I guess that's what I'm thinking."

* * * * *

Lovely called Jaimee on his cell and arranged to meet with her. Then he drove to Tremont Street and called Adrienne. She hurried out of her office and climbed into his car, an anxious expression on her face. She smelled of smoke.

"What did you find out?" she asked.

"It was Andrew Winthrop who told Moore to give keys to Vermino's man. I believe it's the Chosen Few who are after David, not your husband by himself."

"So maybe Marshall doesn't know about David and me."

"Maybe not."

She sighed. "I guess I should be relieved, but I'm too worried about David."

"The best thing you can do is put him in touch with me if he contacts you."

"I'll try."

"Will you be in your office tomorrow?" Lovely asked.

"From nine to twelve."

"I'd like to stop by with a counter-surveillance expert to check your phone. It won't take long, and we can be discreet."

Adrienne agreed. She was silent for a minute, staring out the window. A priest walked by looking somber in his black suit and clerical collar. "It's been a hard day," she said, "a horrible day. But I'm glad I told you about David and me. I've felt so alone not being able to talk to anyone."

"You can talk to me anytime."

"Thank you." She hesitated for a moment, then put her arms around him and hugged him. "Thank you," she repeated, head pressed against his shoulder, with such heartfelt gratitude it brought tears to his eyes.

CHAPTER TWENTY-SEVEN

Lovely climbed the stairs to Jaimee's apartment, trailing his fingers on the silky-smooth mahogany banister. She met him at the door, dressed in denim cut-offs and a white halter top. Each time he visited her, she seemed to be wearing less. Lovely put his finger to his lips and motioned her out into the hall. He closed the door behind them.

"We have to talk out here?" she asked.

"Just to be safe."

She shivered. "I hate this." She sat down cross-legged on the carpeted floor. Lovely sat down beside her. Before he could begin to speak, her expression brightened. "Let's go somewhere, ok?"

"Where?"

"Let's drive over to South Boston and walk on the beach."

Lovely lowered the old Chrysler's convertible top and they crossed the Broadway Bridge to South Boston. It was the most thoroughly Irish neighborhood in the city, famous for its Saint Patrick's Day parade—and its hostility to minorities. Broadway was lined with an assortment of three, four, and five-story buildings, some frame, some brick, most dating from the nineteenth century. School had just let out at South Boston High and teenagers thronged the sidewalks, backpacks slung over their shoulders, books under their arms. A stocky youth in a Semper Fi T-shirt caught sight of Jaimee and did a whiplashing double take. He walked straight into a parking meter.

They drove half a mile to the L Street Beach and parked. The beach was deserted. The water was not yet warm enough for swimming nor the weather for sunbathing. A breeze blew in from the Harbor, carrying the scent of the ocean. Light surf lapped at the sand. They walked east, toward Pleasure Bay.

"I'm ready to listen," Jaimee said.

Lovely told her the story of the Chosen Few. When he finished, she walked in silence for a long time, eyes fixed in front of her. An endless, undulating line of seaweed marked the level of a recent high tide. Up ahead, the old fort on Castle Island came into view.

"I don't believe it," she said. "And yet I do. I mean, it's hard to believe it was all going on and I knew nothing about it. But I always had the feeling there were things David was hiding from me, and it's just like him to dream up a scheme like that—a little gang of geniuses who would take over the world. Why did the group hire mobsters to kill him?"

"I don't know yet. He must have had a disagreement with them over something."

"God. It's horrible to think Andrew and Keith would do something like that—and all over some stupid club."

"Zealots can't stand dissent. It forces them to question their actions and beliefs."

She glanced at him. "Zealots?"

"Sorry. These guys make me think of the Puritans, the way they proclaim their success to be a mark of divine favor— 'the Chosen Few.' The Puritans used to get rid of heretics by hanging them on Boston Common."

Jaimee sighed. "I don't understand how people can be so cruel."

"All is permitted when it's done in the name of God."

When they reached the causeway to Castle Island, Jaimee took off her shoes and waded a few yards into the surf. She stood and stared out at Dorchester Bay, shoes dangling from her hands. From the back, her halter top was just a few strings. Her shorts were cut off right below the pockets. They fit her well. Her legs looked as smooth as the banister in her hallway. She turned around and caught Lovely's eye. She smiled her peculiar smile that projected as much sadness as joy.

"Let's go back," she said. She came out of the surf, put

her shoes in one hand, and slipped her free arm through Lovely's. They headed toward L Street, three-quarters of a mile away.

"Ceci loves the beach," Jaimee said. "She stands by the water's edge, and when a wave breaks, runs screaming away from it. Then she goes back and does it again. I want you to meet her. Can we bring her here tomorrow?"

"I'd love to, but I don't know about tomorrow. This case is picking up speed, and I have a lot to do."

She cast a sideways glance at him. "Are you another man who's headed for destruction?"

"I'm trying not to be."

By the time they reached the car, the wind had picked up. The air felt damp and smelled of salt, and the temperature was dropping. They drove back to the South End through thickening traffic.

"Would you like to come in?" Jaimee asked.

Lovely hesitated. He glanced at the dashboard clock. It was past four, and a Friday.

"I can't. I have to talk to Andrew Winthrop, and I don't want him disappearing on his yacht for the weekend before I get to him."

"Are you going to tell him what you know?"

Lovely nodded.

Jaimee squeezed his hand. "Be careful."

She got out of the car and hurried up the tall stone steps in front of her building. A UPS delivery man, admiring the cut of her shorts, walked into a No Parking sign.

CHAPTER TWENTY-EIGHT

Lovely left the South End and headed across town through rush-hour traffic. He liked Jaimee Kantor a lot. She was completely authentic—unaffected, unpretentious. She was relaxed, easy to talk to, and very easy to look at. She valued simplicity, and she had enchanting sad eyes. She was also his client, and romantically involved with Roland Moore, who was himself entangled in the snarl Lovely was struggling to unravel. It would make his job easier, Lovely decided, if Jaimee would wear more clothes.

He picked up Charles Street and headed north toward Beacon Hill. He didn't expect his encounter with Andrew Winthrop to be pleasant, and he didn't expect Winthrop to tell him the truth. But he needed to see Winthrop's reaction. He had to test his hypothesis that the Chosen Few wanted David Kantor dead.

As Lovely inched along the congested street, there was a break in traffic in the oncoming lane. A Porsche pulled out from behind him and zoomed past, cutting in two cars ahead. The driver would get wherever he was going faster than Lovely. A couple cars here, a couple there; beat the light at the intersection, push the speed limit on the parkway, and when it's over, you reach your destination ten minutes earlier. Or maybe not. Willfullness didn't always produce the desired results. Maybe the man would pull out in front of a truck and wind up with his dashboard in his lap.

Andrew Winthrop's gray Jaguar was not in front of his townhouse, and no one answered the doorbell. Lovely took a seat on the grass, his back against an old elm. The cool breeze blowing in off the bay had reached Beacon Hill. He buttoned up his jacket. An elegant, silver-haired woman in a navy blue dress walked past, looking at him curiously.

"I'm waiting for Godot," he said.

She laughed. "Well, you won't find him here."

An hour and a half later, Winthrop's Jaguar came purring down the cobblestone street. Lovely vaulted the park fence as Winthrop was locking up his car.

"Excuse me."

Winthrop glanced over his shoulder. From the change in his expression, he might have just discovered a worm in his caviar. He turned away. "I don't have time to talk to you." He strode toward his front door.

"When you find out what I have to tell you, you'll make time. You might say it's a matter of life and death."

Winthrop hesitated.

"Let me put it this way," Lovely said. "Would you rather talk about the Chosen Few out here or in there?"

Winthrop's body went rigid. After a moment, he said, "I will listen to what you have to say."

They entered his parlor. Winthrop seated Lovely on the carved rosewood chair beneath the stern gaze of the former ambassador to Great Britain.

Lovely said, "I know that you, David, Keith Riordan, Marshall Forest, and Jeffrey Zimmer made a pact to help each other succeed—a pact for life. I also know that Zimmer and his father represent the Vermino crime family, and that Alessandro Vermino has given an order to have David killed. In fact, one of Vermino's men made a failed attempt the day David disappeared. With David missing, Vermino can't finish his job. So you arranged to have a tall, thin man bug Jaimee's apartment and David's condo. The only thing I don't know is what David did to prompt the Chosen Few to sentence him to death."

Winthrop's face was pale but also hostile. "That is absurd. The Chosen Few had nothing to do with David's disappearance, and we've never had any dealings with mobsters. Jeffrey Zimmer is a highly respected defense attorney. He is well known among his peers for his scrupulous observance of the law. In America, everyone has the right to legal counsel, even those whom we find abhorrent. The fact that Zimmer defends such people does not make him one—except in the eyes of the prejudiced and the ignorant."

Lovely raised his eyebrows. "No wonder you made *Law Review*."

"I beg your pardon?"

"You don't deny hiring the thin man?"

"As I said yesterday, I have a large sum of money on loan to David Kantor. I have every reason to want to locate him."

Lovely took the bag of RF transmitters out of his pocket and held them up. "These are the bugs the thin man planted in Jaimee's apartment. This particular type is available only to law enforcement agencies, but professional criminals can buy them on the black market. Your thin man is a mobster."

Winthrop cast a nervous glance at the bugs. "He assured me he operated entirely within the law. If he's used illegal devices, which I doubt, it was done without my knowledge."

"All right, since you're innocent of any wrongdoing, I'd like you to give me the man's name and phone number so I can have a chat with him."

Winthrop stiffened. His eyes darted away for a second. "I can't give you that information. His contract requires that his identity be kept secret to protect him from retribution. People don't appreciate being eavesdropped upon."

"Show me the contract. You can white out the places where his name appears."

"It's none of your business."

Lovely shook his head. "You and I both know your story is BS. There is no contract. The man's a mobster. He tried to wire my place too, but I ran him off before he could break in. Were you aware of that?"

"I don't know anything about it."

"And then there's the case of the missing files. The thin man must have told you my assistant was going to look through David's file cabinet. Worried it might contain information about the Chosen Few, you had the thin man empty it."

"I don't know what you're talking about," Winthrop said. He glanced at his watch. "I'm afraid I've given you all the time I can spare."

Lovely sighed. "Mr. Winthrop, let me appeal to your common sense. Call off Vermino's men and let this end quietly. That way, you and the Chosen Few can stay out of jail. It's not too late."

Winthrop looked back at him with his trademark expression of irritable contempt. There was something else, there, too—some kind of unshakeable determination that was beyond reason.

"Good night, Mr. Lovely." He rose to his feet and showed Lovely to the door.

CHAPTER TWENTY-NINE

The last sliver of sun sank below the horizon as Lovely made his way home on Soldiers Field Road. He was watching his rear view mirror. He drove slowly down his street, scanning the block, and parked in his stand-alone garage. The little building had an overhead door, but Lovely never bothered to close it. He tugged on it and it squealed, showering him with crud. He stepped outside and pulled it shut.

Years ago, when Lovely had first moved in, his landlord had given him a key to the door. He rummaged through his desk until he found it, went outside, and locked the overhead door. He didn't want his car winding up in a Chelsea junkyard beside the charred remains of Francine Cheyette's van—especially if it burst into flames while he was in it.

Back inside, Lovely checked his windows and rear door. They were all secure. He fed Cyrus and the fish and dropped into his swivel chair. He breathed into the sensation in his gut. The feeling reminded him of a dream he sometimes had that he was driving down a steep hill with no brakes.

He stared at the telephone, thinking how much he would like to hand the case over to the police. But he didn't know what crimes David had committed, and Jaimee was his client. She didn't want her daughter's father going to jail, or becoming a permanent fugitive, or getting killed in a shoot-out with the law. Besides, Lovely had nothing at this point but theories, unproven allegations. He had no evidence that the Chosen Few had hired Vermino to kill David. He couldn't even explain their motive. Only David could give the police the information they would need to bring down the Chosen

Few. Everything hinged on finding him before Vermino silenced him for good.

Lovely fiddled with his ring. He was finding it tolerable. Now he'd have to install the safety device on his spare gun, too. That could wait until he finished the case.

Lovely glanced at his watch. He hadn't eaten in eight hours. The matzoh and peanut butter were gone, which left nothing but condiments. He'd have to go make a run to Star Market, but at the moment, he had no appetite. He changed into sweats and carried his shoulder holster and gun into the living room.

Lovely had furnished one corner of the room with a weight bench and a rack of barbells. He hung his holster on the rack and put two 45-pound plates on the olympic bar. He lay down on the bench and pressed the bar ten times, breathing rhythmically. He did six sets on the bench then moved on to the curl bar, inhaling as he let the bar down, exhaling as he pulled it up. With each set, his mind settled more deeply into the present. After curls, he lay down backwards on the bench and did six sets behind his head for his triceps, and another six straight up from his solar plexus, breathing in, breathing out. He finished with standing military presses. The leg exercises would wait until tomorrow. Lovely showered and dressed. As he was pulling on a T-shirt, the doorbell rang.

He went to the living room window and glanced out at the porch. A person stood at his front door, but he couldn't see who in the darkness. He turned on the porch light and went back to the window. It was a woman with long brown hair and a black mini-dress with slits up the side. Her skin was very tan, and there was a lot of it showing. But that didn't mean she hadn't been sent by Vermino. She rang the bell again, casting an anxious glance down the street. Lovely could see both her hands. She wasn't carrying a gun and had no place to conceal one. He went to the door and opened it.

"I'm Judy Winter," she said in a shaky voice. She spoke with a slight southern accent. "I called yesterday about the stalker."

Lovely remembered. The one who sounded like a ticking bomb.

"He's *there*," she said.

"Where?"

"On the street, in a car." She gestured with her head.

Lovely looked past her through the twilight. A dark-colored sedan was parked beside the curb, a hundred feet away.

"He followed me from the Back Bay," she said. Her lip was trembling. "I didn't know what to do. I had your address in my handbag so I came here. I'm sorry." Her voice cracked.

"That's all right." Lovely glanced up and down the street. It was a neighborhood where people parked in their garages. The only other car in sight was a white Honda Civic, parked in front of Lovely's walkway. It appeared to be unoccupied.

"That your Honda?" he asked.

She nodded.

"Wait here." He descended the porch steps and headed down the street toward the stalker's sedan. As he drew near it, Lovely could see the man's visor was lowered. There was no reason for it at this hour, except to hide his face. Something squeezed in Lovely's gut. It was a trap. The stalker was the prowler, or Joe Brenna, or the puffy-faced kid the Ant had roughed up. Lovely thought of his Ruger, hanging on the weight rack in his living room.

The car's engine roared to life. Lovely froze. The driver was going to run him down. He glanced around, searching for an escape route. There were no cars on the street, no trees on the sidewalk, no cover of any kind. The car lurched into gear. The engine revved and it sped away backwards down the street.

Lovely let out his breath. "Jesus."

At the end of the block, the car U-turned and drove out of sight. Lovely shook himself. He was getting paranoid. He walked back to the porch, knees wobbly.

"You all right?" he asked Judy.

"I guess so. Just a little shaken up." She looked the way

Lovely felt. "I'm really sorry about showing up like this."

"That's ok. Come on in."

He held the door for her and she passed into the house. She smelled of perfume, and something else—a faint chemical smell that was vaguely familiar. Some kind of nail polish, maybe, or hair spray.

"Please excuse the mess," Lovely said.

She glanced around the room and froze. Lovely followed her gaze. She was staring at his holster and gun.

"Don't worry," he said quickly. "It won't hurt you."

He stowed it in the hall closet beside his spare and seated Judy on the couch. She was in her mid twenties, he guessed, very attractive, with large brown eyes and full lips. Her dress was cut low on her breasts and high on her thighs. She was maybe ten pounds overweight, but it didn't make her look fat, just ripe. Her knee was bouncing like a jackhammer.

"What happened?" he asked.

Her words came out in a torrent. "I walked out of my apartment and got into my car. I drove around the corner and stopped at a red light on Boylston Street. There was a car right behind me. Then it pulled up beside me and there he was, grinning at me."

"Did you get his plate number?"

"No, I wasn't thinking. I just wanted to get away as fast as I could. I don't even know what kind of car it was. I think it was blue." She crossed her legs and began jiggling her foot.

"Has he ever followed you in a car before?"

"No. And my Honda was parked right in front of my building, so he must have seen me come out. He must have been waiting for me. He knows where I live, now, and what car I drive. I know you said on the phone you were busy, but I wonder if..." She looked imploringly at Lovely.

He shook his head. "I'm very, very sorry, but there's just no way I can take your case right now. I'm involved with something that would make it impossible. I'll be glad to work for you as soon as I finish."

Her shoulders sagged.

"Irene wasn't able to refer you to anyone else?" Lovely

asked.

"I left a message for her, but she hasn't called back."

"Can't you get someone to stay with you in the meantime?"

"I'll ask my brother. He's in New York on business, but he'll be back in the morning." She glanced at him uncertainly. "Do you think...could I possibly...stay here until then?"

Lovely hesitated only for a second. It was tempting, but out of the question. "I'm very sorry, but I'm having a serious problem with some people and it wouldn't be safe for you here. Can't you stay with a friend?"

"I just moved here last month. I don't really know anyone except my brother."

"Oh."

There was an uncomfortable silence. Her foot started jiggling again. "Maybe I can get him to come home tonight instead of tomorrow. Can I use your phone?"

"Of course."

Lovely showed her to his desk and returned to the living room. He dropped onto the couch. Her manic energy was irritating. But there was something erotic about it, too. She kept squirming in her seat.

Cyrus came slinking out of the bedroom, casting resentful backward glances. He hopped up on the couch. Lovely could hear Judy speaking on the phone: "Bruce Winter, please... Thank God you're there. That stalker followed me in his car tonight." She repeated the story she had told Lovely and made some arrangements with her brother. She came back into the room. Cyrus looked up at her and hissed.

"Don't worry," Lovely said. "He does that to everyone. What did your brother say?"

"He can't make it till the morning, so I'm going to stay in a hotel. I have nothing to do for the next few hours but sit in a room watching television. Can't I take you out to dinner as thanks for saving me from that man?"

Lovely hesitated again, just long enough to douse the hotel-room image that darted into his mind.

"It's a nice offer, but I better not. What I really need to

do is make a run to Star Market for groceries and get some sleep."

"I understand."

"Call me next week and we'll get to work on that stalker."

"All right. May I use your bathroom before I go?"

"Of course."

When she came out, Lovely walked her to the front hall and opened the door for her. She stopped in front of him, barely a foot away, and looked up at him. "Thank you."

Her dress was held up by two little strings. It was slightly less sheer than a veil. Lovely wondered, vaguely, if bras had gone out of fashion. She smiled at him. The voice in Lovely's head told him to get her out the door.

"You're welcome," he said, and he held out his hand. She took it but didn't shake it. Her eyes were on his face.

"Good night," he said with as much firmness as he could muster. It wasn't much.

"I don't have to leave, you know."

"It's not safe for you here."

"Then come with me."

Lovely hesitated.

She smiled at him. "You want to, don't you?" She stepped forward and kissed him.

Lovely's head began to pound. Her tongue reached into his mouth, tentatively at first, searching for his. It tasted like mint. She was still holding his hand, her plump fingers pressing into his palm, the pressure increasing as their kiss grew more heated. She slid his hand up her torso and onto her breast. A little sighing sound came from her throat. Lovely could feel her nipple harden under his finger tips.

Outside, a breeze blew, creaking the hinges of the open door. Lovely's mind cleared for a moment. He drew his head back and studied her face. "Why are you doing this?"

She looked startled. Then she laughed a little laugh that sounded forced. "Why do you think?"

"I don't know. Tell me."

"Because I like what I see in front of me."

144

She was lying.

"Good night," Lovely said. "Call me next week." He put his hands on her bare shoulders, turned her gently around, and guided her through the door. He closed it behind her and locked it. Through the window, he watched her climb into her Honda Civic and drive away.

Lovely sat down on the couch and waited for his heartbeat to return to normal. Had she been sent by Vermino after all? Would she have stabbed him in his sleep with a knife from the kitchen, or gone out to her car for her handbag and smuggled in a pistol? He shuddered. If so, she was a very good actor. He thought back to her story about the stalker. It had been very convincing. But Lovely had been somewhat dazed by his encounter with the man in the car, so he hadn't been paying the closest attention. And then there was that tiny dress: very distracting. He wished he had asked her some questions about her life. He would have been able to tell pretty quickly if she were lying. She had been at the end, he was certain of that. But the truth might have been nothing malevolent. Maybe she wanted to go to bed with him because she was frightened and didn't want to be alone. Or maybe not.

Lovely glanced at his watch. He had to eat, which meant he had to shop. He took his gun out of the closet and strapped it on, covering it with a windbreaker. He went out the back door and pulled it shut behind him. It was a self-locking door, but he checked it, just to be sure.

Traffic was light on Mount Auburn Street. Lovely kept one eye on the rear-view mirror. When he reached Star Market, he parked in the fire lane in front of the entrance. He spent twenty minutes wandering up and down the aisles, and another twenty getting through the check-out. He paused at the exit, scanning the parking lot, then loaded his groceries into his trunk. No one followed him home. There were no strange cars parked on his street and no prowlers on his porch. He parked in the garage, locked it, and carried his bags in through the back door. A quick check of the windows found them all locked and unbroken. He'd be very glad when this was over.

As Lovely was putting away his groceries, it occurred to him that he could ask Irene Freeman if she had referred Judy to him, as Judy had claimed. He called the Women's Crisis Center, which stayed open late, but was told Irene would not be in until Monday. Lovely hung up and leaned back in his chair, thinking about the radio frequency bug Francine had removed from Jaimee's living room wall. Vermino's eavesdroppers would have overheard Jaimee and Lovely talking about Irene during their first meeting. Was that how Judy came up with Irene's name? Lovely ate a meal without tasting it and went to sleep with his gun beside his bed.

CHAPTER THIRTY

Oz was sitting on the edge of the roof on Tremont Street, feet dangling, watching the traffic move up and down the street. Each year there were more cars, and the cars were more expensive. Oz had an old Chevy pick-up for hauling his tools and supplies, but he left it parked when he wasn't working. He traveled around Boston the way it was meant to be traveled: by streetcar and by foot.

Down below, a white BMW cruised past and rounded the corner onto a side street. The car looked vaguely familiar. Oz heard a sharp whistle from the other direction and turned to look for the source. Three teen-age boys were strutting down the sidewalk. Their pants were as baggy as laundry sacks and half a foot too long. The whistler raised a hand to Oz.

"What do you say, Willy?" Oz called down to him.

A lone white man coming along the sidewalk toward the boys discreetly crossed the street. Oz smiled wryly. Those three weren't bad, but they did look mean. It was all part of surviving in the inner-city schools. If you looked tough, people were less likely to mess with you.

Oz heard a sound on the roof and glanced over. A yellow rectangle of light was visible fifty yards away. The door of the head house on the last building had just opened. The door closed, and Oz saw a figure coming across the rooftops. Now he remembered why the white BMW looked familiar. He lay down flat on the roof.

David Kantor walked past him, climbed over the railing to Jaimee's roof deck, and disappeared down the stairs to her balcony. Oz rose lightly to his feet and hurried along the roof to the head house. He pulled on the door and it opened.

147

Apparently, David had not noticed the piece of tape Oz had put over the latch. Oz ran down four flights of stairs and out the front entrance. He turned the corner onto the side street and spotted the BMW parked beneath a streetlight. He paused. He had no cell phone. He could call Lovely from a pay phone, but there wasn't much chance Lovely would make it in from Watertown in time to catch David.

Oz sprinted down Tremont Street toward Massachusetts Avenue, three blocks away. The teenagers he had seen from the roof turned around at the sound of his footsteps and stepped aside as he raced past. Oz turned the corner and ran up the stone steps of a brick townhouse. He rang the bell for apartment two.

After a minute, the intercom squawked. An old woman with a heavy Spanish accent said, "Who is it?"

"It's Oz, *Abuelita*. Let me in."

The door released and Oz ran up a flight of stairs. His grandmother opened the door, dressed in a nightgown and slippers. She was only five-foot-two, but she seemed much bigger.

"What do you think you're doing ringing my bell at this time of night?" she demanded.

"It's only ten o'clock and it's an emergency. I need to borrow your car."

"Not on your life."

"Come on, I ain't got time to mess with you."

"The last time I lent you my car..."

"That was fifteen years ago. I'll have it back in an hour—two at the most."

She looked at him sharply. "What kind of trouble are you getting yourself into, Osmond Quinn?"

"I'll explain later. Just give me the keys."

"*Ay Dios mijo*," she muttered, shaking her head. "You'll be the death of me, Osmond." She went into the apartment and returned with her keys. "It's parked across the street. If you don't have it back by midnight, I'll skin you alive."

"Thanks." He ran down the stairs and across the street. The car was a glossy-black Buick Riviera, twelve years old but immaculately maintained. He climbed in behind the wheel.

"Take your time, David," Oz muttered. "Watch your little girl." He pulled away from the curb, tires squealing, and raced around the corner to the side street where David had parked. The BMW still sat by the curb. Oz drove past it and parked in front of a hydrant at the end of the block. He ran back to the BMW.

Oz took a lock knife out of his pocket and jammed the blade into the lens of David's taillight. "Sorry, David." Two more stabs and a half-dollar-sized chunk of red plastic fell out onto the pavement. Oz went back to the Buick. Five minutes later, David walked around the corner. He climbed into his car and pulled away from the curb. Oz slid down in his seat as David drove past, then started his engine and went after him. As a result of Oz's handiwork, David had one red taillight and one white one. Oz could identify the car from a quarter mile away.

David drove down Massachusetts Avenue to the Turnpike and headed west. Traffic was light. Oz hung way back, watching the BMW's lights. Ten miles out of Boston, David left the Pike and headed north on I-95. At Route Two, he turned west again. They passed Walden Pond and Concord, leaving the suburbs behind. The highway ran through hay fields, orchards, and woods.

Fifty miles west of Boston, David left Route Two and headed north on a country road. Oz was confident he had not been noticed yet, but now he was at risk. There were no other cars on the road, and he would have to follow David more closely on the twisting road to avoid losing him. He moved up to within two hundred yards of the BMW and hoped for the best.

Five miles south of the New Hampshire border, just past a village called Ashton, Oz came around a bend and was confronted by a crossroads. David's car was not in sight. Oz made a flash decision to go straight. He stepped on the gas. Forty-five, fifty, sixty. He was sailing down the winding road, testing the outer limits of the Buick's handling. When he reached the New Hampshire line, he backed off the gas.

Obviously, David had turned right or left at the crossroads. Oz glanced at the clock. Eleven-fifteen; he was already going to be past his curfew. He U-turned and headed for home.

CHAPTER THIRTY-ONE

A light morning mist clung to the ground when Lovely left his apartment by the back way. The grass glistened with dew. He checked the garage door and found it secure, with no signs of tampering. Inside, he opened the Chrysler's hood and inspected the engine with a flashlight, then slid beneath the car and examined the undercarriage. Everything appeared to be normal. He climbed into the driver's seat and depressed the accelerator once to set the choke. Gritting his teeth, he turned the key. The car started without exploding. Lovely took a few deep breaths, backed out, and locked the garage.

Francine Cheyette had agreed, reluctantly, to sweep David's apartment that day. The only time she could spare was between eight and nine a.m., so Lovely found himself in the unfamiliar position of driving into Boston at seven-thirty on a Saturday morning. He met Francine on West Canton Street, and they spent an hour in David's condominium. They found two RF transmitters, identical to those they had removed from Jaimee's apartment. When they finished, they stopped by Adrienne's office to check her telephone. It was clean. Francine headed back to Chelsea, and Lovely took Adrienne into the conference room.

"I want to talk to your husband about the Chosen Few."

Adrienne's eyes opened wide. "What for?!"

"I need to find out why the group is after David, and I don't have any other leads."

"He won't tell you anything."

"Maybe not, but there's always the chance he'll let some information slip out. There's another reason I need to talk to him, too: Andrew Winthrop knows I found out about the Chosen Few. I don't want him or your husband to suspect you were my source. I made up a story to explain how I came by the information, and I need someone to tell it to."

She shook her head uneasily. "I'm not sure visiting him is a good idea. Can't you call him instead?"

"It's too hard to read people over the phone. Is he home now?"

"As far as I know. I'm meeting him back there at twelve-thirty. He was in a dark mood when I left—and last night, too."

"My conversation with Winthrop was pretty tense," Lovely said. "He probably spoke to Marshall."

She nodded. "Andrew did call last night, but Marshall was brooding even before that. There's something else going on."

"Any idea what?"

"No, and I probably won't ask. It's best to keep out of his way when he's in one of those moods. Maybe you should talk to him tomorrow."

"He won't be any happier to see me then."

"Are you going to phone him first?"

"No, I think it'll be safer if he's not expecting me."

Adrienne shook her head again. "Be careful. Don't make him angry."

"I'll try not to."

* * * * *

Marshall Forest lived in a hilly neighborhood of Newton, a suburb ten miles west of Boston. Lovely drove along the twisting streets past three-story Victorian houses with leaded-glass windows and porte cocheres. A Rottweiler on a chain barked at his car. Two doors down, a boy in his early teens was washing a pair of Mercedes sedans, one white, one midnight blue.

Forest's house was an imposing English Tudor painted a yellowish beige with dark brown trim. Giant oaks lined the street and shadowed the front yard. Lovely parked in the driveway beside an iron lamp post. He walked up the

152

flagstone path to the front entrance and rang the bell. Forest came to the door. He was about Lovely's height, powerfully built, with black hair and dark, deep-set eyes. He looked as mirthless as Adrienne. Lovely introduced himself and handed Forest a business card. Forest glanced at it. His gaze shifted to Lovely's old Chrysler, where it lingered.

"Come in."

Lovely stepped through the door into a long hall. To his left, a doorway opened into the living room. To his right, a stairway led up to the second floor, curving as it rose above the level of the hall. There was a four-foot section of blank wall at the foot of the stairs, partially covered by an Oriental tapestry decorated with wild animals and flowering trees.

Lovely heard the door click shut and he turned around to face his host. Marshall's face contorted into a snarl. He let out a gurgle of rage and grabbed Lovely by the throat. In the same unbroken motion, he ran Lovely backward the width of the entrance hall and slammed his head against the wall at the foot of the stairs. The force was so great, the plaster beneath the tapestry cracked. A shower of dust and debris fell to the floor at Lovely's feet. He heard it from far away. His mind felt like a boat slowly spinning in a dense fog. His body was limp.

"I saw her in your car yesterday," he heard Forest growl in a distant voice. "I saw your little goodbye. It's been going on for months, hasn't it?"

Lovely tried to say no, but he couldn't stop the spinning in his head. He felt Forest's hands tighten on his throat, squeezing his windpipe. Lovely's breathing stopped. The spinning in his head slowed. He felt it halt, as if the boat had bumped into a rock. His lungs were aching. His vision cleared enough for him to see the outline of Forest's face, inches from his own. Then the lack of oxygen overtook him and Forest's face blurred and disappeared. Lovely sagged against the wall.

Forest's grip loosened and Lovely felt a trickle of air pass through his windpipe. He took a slow breath, and another, shallow and stealthy, and two more. Then he jammed his knee into Forest's groin.

Forest fell onto the floor, clutching his testicles. Lovely

leaned back against the tapestry, breathing and waiting for his mind to clear. When it did, he sat down heavily on the stairs and drew his gun. He touched the back of his head with his free hand. A lump was rising.

"I'm not having an affair with your wife, Marshall. I only met her yesterday. She hugged me because she was grateful. We had just been through an intense series of conversations. I know all about the Chosen Few and your plan to kill David Kantor, as I'm sure you heard from Andrew Winthrop. I told Adrienne about the plot and threatened to go to the police if she didn't cooperate with me. In the end, she agreed to try to persuade you to call off Vermino's men. I stopped by her office this morning for a report. She told me you were in an angry mood last night and she was afraid to confront you. So I came instead, never guessing you'd try to knock down a wall with my head."

It was another minute before Forest was able to haul himself to a sitting position. He looked pallid and shaky. "How do you know about the Chosen Few?"

"I found a file full of papers hidden in David's bedroom closet. Unfortunately, there was nothing to explain why you're trying to kill him."

"We're not trying to kill him," Marshall said woodenly.

Lovely raised a hand to silence him. "Listen, Marshall: I'm trying to save David's life, not ruin yours. Maybe we can work out something that will allow him to live, and allow you and your *Law Review* buddies to stay out of prison."

"I don't know what you're talking about."

Lovely groaned. "You guys are so goddamn mule-headed, I'd pound my head against the wall if you hadn't done it for me. Would you have some sense just this one time? It's not too late to avoid disaster."

"Get out of my house," Forest said quietly. "And don't come back."

He did. As soon as Lovely was out of sight of the driveway, he called Adrienne and told her the story he had given her husband. She wrote it down, word for word.

CHAPTER THIRTY-TWO

Lovely rounded a bend and passed the teenaged boy, still at work on the Mercedes sedans. Two doors down, the Rottweiler was at his post, guarding his master's worldly possessions. Lovely didn't know any more about the Chosen Few than he had ten minutes earlier. The only change was the lump on the back of his head and the plaster dust on his shoes.

A mile down the road, the cell phone rang. It was Lieutenant Thomas.

"I think I found your cabby, Max. His name is Terrance Gallagher. Drives for Town Taxi. A man climbed into his cab in front of the Marriott Hotel around two-thirty a.m. Friday morning, out of breath."

"That has to be him. Where did they go?"

"Tremont Street in the South End."

"I'm not surprised. Did the cabby get an address?"

"No. But he said he might recognize the place if he saw it. You want to take him for a drive down Tremont?"

"Where does he live?"

"Brighton."

Lovely U-turned. "Give me his phone number."

Like most of Boston's outlying neighborhoods, Brighton had once been an agricultural community. A cattle market had been established there during the Revolutionary War, and the town became known for its stockyards. The arrival of the railroad, and later the trolley, had spurred residential development in the pattern typical of the region: first single-family homes, then as land became scarce, row houses, triple-deckers, and apartment buildings. Eventually, the city of Boston annexed Brighton. It was now a mix of students, young professionals, and European, Asian, and Latin American immigrants.

Terrence Gallagher lived above a Greek restaurant on a

busy street lined with brick row houses. Lovely honked his horn and Gallagher came out the door. He was in his mid-twenties, with a goatee and sunglasses.

"Thanks for taking the time to help me out," Lovely said as they drove away.

"No problem. You a real P.I.?"

"Yes."

The second question always followed the first, like thunder after lightning.

"Carry a gun?"

"Yes."

The third question was less certain—like the crash sound that sometimes followed the screech of tires. Not everyone wanted to know the answer. Lovely could feel Gallagher weighing the question—*have you ever shot anyone?* He didn't ask it. Maybe he sensed how intensely personal it was.

Lovely said. "Tell me about the guy you drove from the Marriott Hotel."

"He jumped in, out of breath, and said, 'Tremont Street. I'm in a hurry.' I turned right on Dartmouth Street and right again when we reached Tremont. We didn't go far from there—half a dozen blocks, maybe, and he got out. Not even a five-minute ride, start to finish. He gave me a ten-dollar bill and told me to keep the change."

"Did you see him go into a building?"

Gallagher paused to consider the question. "I didn't wait around to watch him open the door, but I remember him walking straight across the sidewalk. I'm sure he was going in."

"Did you talk to him at all?"

"No, a guy like that—breathing hard and in a big hurry in the middle of the night? There was something menacing about him, too. He had this steely voice." Gallagher shook his head. "I kept quiet."

"What did he look like?"

Gallagher paused again. "Couldn't tell you. He sat in the back seat and handed me the cash through the partition. I wasn't paying any more attention to him than I had to. What did he do, if you don't mind my asking?"

"Strangled my next-door neighbor."

Gallagher went rigid. He was silent for a moment, then he shook his head. "Guess I called him right."

"Yeah, you did."

They turned the corner onto Tremont Street. After a few blocks, Gallagher said, "Slow down." He scanned the buildings lining the street. "I wonder if he's home."

When they reached the block across from Jaimee's, Gallagher said, "This could be it."

Lovely stopped the car. "Which building?"

Gallagher scanned the row of townhouses. "Can you tell them apart?"

They were all identical.

"And the next block's the same. Could be either one."

Lovely grimaced. "Was it an end building?"

"I don't think so. That leaves you a couple hundred people to sift through."

"Yeah. Would you recognize him?"

"Not likely. Wouldn't you?"

Lovely shook his head. "Didn't see his face."

"I guess I wasn't much help."

Lovely shrugged. "It may pay off. I'll report it to the detectives investigating the murder. Maybe they can canvas the buildings." He pressed a fifty-dollar bill into Gallagher's hand and drove him back to Brighton.

CHAPTER THIRTY-THREE

Lovely locked his car in the garage, checked the windows and doors in his apartment, and dropped into his swivel chair. A flashing light on the telephone indicated a new message.

"Wake up, Mister Lovely, it's Oz calling at eight-thirty Saturday morning. I followed David Kantor last night. Call me."

Oz told Lovely the story of his drive out to north-central Massachusetts in his grandmother's Buick. "I lost him at a crossroads just north of a town called Ashton. Ever heard of it?"

"No."

"Doubt anyone else has, either. He must be staying near the place—there'd be no reason for him to drive on that little country road if he was going any distance."

Lovely hung up and dialed Jaimee's cell phone. "Can you walk outside and call me back?"

"Right now?"

"Yes."

"Well...ok."

She got back to him a minute later. Lovely told her the story of Oz's trip. "Does David have any friends in that part of the state, or any other reason to go there?"

"Not that I know of..." She paused. "But it does remind me of one thing: he used to talk about vacations he took with his family on some lake when he was a kid. I remember him saying it was just a few miles from New Hampshire. They used to stay in a cabin. The place had a kind of exotic name..." She was silent for a minute. "Eden Lake. That's what it was."

"I'll look it up."

Lovely hung up the phone and opened a map of Massachusetts. Eden Lake was just a few miles northwest of Ashton. He ran out to his car.

Lovely drove north to Route Two and headed west. He was watching the mirror again. Three miles south of Lexington, he left the highway and rolled to a stop at the bottom of the exit ramp. One car followed him off. It turned right and headed north toward Lexington center. Lovely waited till it was out of sight.

Just before one p.m., Lovely pulled into the village of Ashton. It consisted of a white frame church with an adjacent cemetery and a matching post office the size of a one-car garage. Lovely parked in front of the post office and walked up to the entrance. The door was locked. A sign in the window said the office closed at noon on Saturdays. A teenage boy was doing three-sixties on his skateboard in the parking lot. He had dyed-red hair, a baggy, untucked, button-down shirt, and a lit cigarette hanging from his mouth. Lovely waved to him.

"Can you tell me how to get to Eden Lake?"

The boy rolled up to him and skidded to a stop. He pointed his cigarette in the direction Lovely had been driving.

"Keep going till you come to a crossroads. Go left, and the lake's like a mile up the road."

"Any cabins up there you can rent by the day or the week?"

"Eden Lake Cabins. You can't miss the sign, it's got an apple and a snake."

The Eden Lake Cabins were set back a hundred yards off a narrow country road. Lovely turned into the gravel driveway and parked in front of an old farmhouse with an "Office" sign over the front door. He climbed out of his car and walked down the driveway toward the water. There were half a dozen cabins spread out along the wooded lake front—one-story frame buildings painted brown, barely large enough to accommodate two rooms. Lovely passed several which appeared to be unoccupied. The drive ended. He spotted the nose of a white BMW Roadster parked on the far side of the last cabin. Lovely walked over to the car. There was a patch of Bondo, unpainted, on the driver's door. It looked like it had been applied by an amateur. The broken window had been replaced.

Lovely went back to the cabin entrance and knocked. The floor creaked inside. He heard hurried movements.

"Who is it?" a man asked.

"My name's Max Lovely. I need to speak to you, David."

After a pause, the man said, "There's no one here by that name." His voice was so tight, it sounded like he was choking.

"I'm a private investigator, David. Your wife is worried about you and hired me to find you. You can call her to verify, but her phone may be tapped, so don't tell her where you are."

Two minutes passed. Lovely heard footsteps approach the door. "Go away," the man said.

Lovely guessed that David had phoned Jaimee, but she had not picked up. Lovely sighed. "I'm not going away, David. I drove an hour and a half to get here and I'm not leaving till I talk to you. I'll camp out on your doorstep if I have to."

There was a pause. "Do you have a gun?"

"Yes."

"Where is it?"

"In a holster under my arm."

"Stand in front of my windows and take the holster off."

Lovely rolled his eyes. He walked over to the cabin windows, which were curtained, and removed his holster. He laid it on the ground and returned to the cabin entrance.

"I'm going to open the door," the man said. "Come in nice and slow with your hands over your head."

The door swung outward and Lovely went in. He stood on the threshold for a moment, waiting for his eyes to adjust to the dim light. When they did, he saw the muzzle of a Smith and Wesson .44 Magnum pointed at his face. David Kantor was holding it awkwardly in both hands. The gun was

160

shaking so badly he might have had palsy.

"For God's sake," Lovely said, "take it easy with that thing."

"Sit on the couch."

It was a rustic pine bench with a wooden back and a cushioned seat. Lovely eased himself onto it. There were two matching armchairs facing it, and in between, a coffee table piled high with copies of the Boston *Globe* and the New England *Real Estate Journal*.

David pulled the door shut. "Put your hands on your knees and keep them there."

Lovely moved his hands to his knees, very slowly. David sat down in an armchair with the trembling .44 Magnum aimed at Lovely's chest. The gun looked brand new.

"You're making me real nervous," Lovely said.

"Sorry, I can't take any chances."

"If you rest the butt on your thigh and loosen your grip a little, your hands won't shake so much. Then maybe it won't go off by accident."

David eased the gun onto his thigh.

Lovely let out his breath. "Thank you."

"What do you want?" David asked. He had lost weight since posing for the photograph Lovely had seen. He was dressed in blue jeans and a wrinkled Oxford shirt.

"Jaimee hired me because she was afraid you might be in trouble and might need help. I've spent the last four days trying to figure out why you dropped out of sight. I've learned a few things. I know about the Chosen Few. I know about Jeffrey Zimmer's connection to Alessandro Vermino, and that Vermino has a contract out on you. I've gotten the death look from Andrew Winthrop, and been knocked around by Marshall Forest. But I still don't know why the Chosen Few are out to kill you. If you'll tell me what's going on, I may still be able to save your life—and mine."

"How did you find me?"

"A friend of mine tailed you from Tremont Street last night."

"Did you tell anyone where I am?"

"No, and I'm sure he didn't, either."

"How did you find out about the Chosen Few?"

"I can't answer that question yet. Maybe later."

"What's this about Jaimee's phone being tapped?"

"I pulled eavesdropping devices out of her telephones and her wall. Your apartment was wired, too."

David's eyes seemed to sink deeper into their sockets.

"These guys aren't messing around," Lovely said. "Winthrop admitted to hiring the man who planted the bugs. I believe that man works for Vermino. Tell me what's going on between you and the other guys in the group."

David chewed on his lip. Then he shook his head. "If I tell you, there's no turning back. I think I can wait it out and fix things up with them...after."

"After what?"

"I can't say."

"The way it looks to me," Lovely said, "there's already no turning back. I've seen the determination on the faces of Winthrop and Forest. You're dreaming if you think you can persuade them to let you live. Your only hope is to take your story to the police. If the Chosen Few knew your death would be blamed on them, they might call off Vermino. You might survive this—as long as you haven't done anything to Vermino himself."

"I haven't. You're sure it's Vermino who's trying to kill me?"

Lovely nodded. "My thug talked to his thug—with a hot fireplace poker."

"Jesus." David eyed Lovely nervously.

"You're up against a nasty bunch of people, David. The only way out is the police."

David hesitated then shook his head again. "I can straighten it out with them after. They're all old friends of mine."

Lovely resisted the urge to groan. "How long will it be until `after?'"

"About a month."

"It's too long. Someone's going to wind up dead. At

162

least tell me your story and I'll keep it a secret as long as you're alive. You're the only one who knows what the Chosen Few are up to. If Vermino gets you, they'll be out of reach of the law."

David was silent for a minute. "I don't know. I'll think it over."

Lovely sighed. He had pushed him as far as he could. "All right. But try to think quick. We're running out of time."

CHAPTER THIRTY-FOUR

Lovely watched the houses grow closer together and the traffic thicken as he made his way back to Boston. He could feel the knot in his stomach tightening. Ten miles from home, Adrienne Forest called. Lovely told her about his meeting with David and asked how things had gone with her husband.

"All right, I guess. I stuck to your story. I don't know if he believed me or not, but it doesn't really matter."

"Why not?"

"I've been doing a lot of thinking, and I've decided to leave him. My heart is with David."

Lovely raised his eyebrows. "How does it feel?"

"Like a hundred pounds has been lifted off my back."

"Glad to hear it." He was trying to sound supportive, but inside, he was wondering if David Kantor would live to enjoy his good fortune.

"I can't stay on the phone," Adrienne said. "I just wanted to tell you about it. You helped me—more than you realize. I'll always be grateful."

The sun was low in the sky when Lovely pulled into his driveway. He went inside and checked the windows and doors, then dropped into his swivel chair. He took out his Ruger and released the cylinder to check the load. He laid the gun on his desk, steel clunking against oak. Sighing, he turned to look at his aquarium.

A school of tiger barbs, yellow, black, and orange, hovered in one corner. They were full of repressed energy, snapping their tail fins every few seconds to stay in place against the current. Below them, a spiny eel was curled up beneath a ceramic footbridge, snout protruding, calm, attentive. An angelfish came out of the branches of an

Amazon sword plant and swam to the front of the tank. Lovely dropped in a pinch of food. The fish's eyes were on the sides of its flat body, which had to make frontal vision difficult, but its aim at the floating flakes was flawless. Water-logged food that sank was snapped up by the tiger barbs. Anything missed by the barbs would be scavenged by the catfish or the spiny eel. The fish's own waste would be consumed by bacteria which would convert it to nitrogen and oxygen. The nitrogen would be absorbed by the aquatic plants, and the oxygen by the fish. Lovely liked his aquarium a lot. Sometimes he wished he lived in a glass-bottomed boat somewhere far away.

It was dusk when Roland Moore called. He sounded uneasy.

"I just got a call from a woman named Judy Winter," Moore said. "She told me she was working for David and wanted to ask some questions about you."

Lovely sat up straight. "Did she have a southern accent?"

"Yeah. You know her?"

"No, but I met her briefly. What did you tell her?"

"Nothing. She asked if she could stop by in an hour, and I agreed. Just thought I ought to let you know."

"She gave me a different story," Lovely said, "so she's lying to one of us—or maybe both. I better come over and wait with you. She may be dangerous."

"Well...all right."

"Did she give you a phone number?"

"No."

Lovely got directions to Moore's house and hung up the phone. She had to be from Vermino. Lovely sat very still, wondering how close he had been to death when he kissed her the night before. He thought back to the time she had spent in his apartment: sitting on the couch, making the phone call to her "brother," using the bathroom. His thoughts turned to the "stalker." He must have been a fake, too—probably another Vermino operative. Could he have been the thin man? A cold feeling filled Lovely's belly. He grabbed a screwdriver from his desk and removed the two Phillips head screws from the bottom of his telephone. He lifted off the plastic cover. A radio frequency device was neatly spliced into the wires.

Lovely grasped it all in an instant: He had mentioned to Judy that he was going to Star Market. Right before she left, when she used the bathroom, she unlocked the window for her "stalker"—the thin man. She probably called him from her car to let him know Lovely would be leaving shortly. One of them must have waited on Mount Auburn Street, the busy thoroughfare that led to the supermarket, watching for Lovely to pass. While Lovely was shopping, the thin man had climbed in and bugged the phone, then relocked the window and let himself out, locking the door behind him. He probably had a receiver hidden in a parked car on Mount Auburn Street, which was well within transmitting distance. They had heard or recorded all the calls Lovely had made in the last twenty-four hours.

Lovely grabbed his cell phone and dialed David's number. The eavesdroppers would have picked up Lovely's conversations with Oz and Jaimee that morning. They knew David was staying in a cabin on Eden Lake, not far from Ashton. That's all the information they would need to find him.

The phone rang once, twice, three times. The cabin only had two rooms. It rang twice more. Lovely was too late. He hung up and called again, unwilling for David to be dead; hoping, desperately, that he had dialed a wrong number. David picked up on the first ring.

Lovely breathed a prayer of thanksgiving. "Do you know a woman named Judy Winter? Brown hair, big eyes, talks with a southern accent, drives a white Honda Civic?"

"No."

"That's what I thought. Get out of that cabin as fast as you can. The bastards tapped my phone. They heard me talk to Jaimee about Eden Lake. They know where you are. Clear out, *now*, and call me on my cell phone in the morning to find out what's going on. Understand?"

"Y...yes.

166

Lovely hung up, stuffed his gun in his holster, and ran out to his car. As he roared off down the street, his phone rang.

Adrienne's voice sounded breathless. "You told me to call you if I thought of anything."

"That's right."

"It's something Marshall told me the night Keith Riordan got elected to his first term. Remember the scandal that brought down the incumbent mayor—his fling with a seventeen-year-old who filmed them in bed?"

"Yes."

"Marshall said to me, with a nasty little smile, `We gave the girl the idea.'"

Lovely whistled. "Did he tell you any details?"

"No, and I didn't ask. That's all I know."

Lovely thanked her and hung up the phone. It didn't take him long to piece together a scenario. The young woman must have been a prostitute hired by the Chosen Few. Zimmer could have found her easily enough with his mob connections. They must have concluded that Riordan was going to lose—he had been trailing until the scandal broke—and decided they couldn't wait another four years. They had surmised, correctly, that Mayor Sullivan would forget his family values when confronted with an eager seventeen-year-old. Since Sullivan had made much of his Christian virtue during the campaign, the scandal had disgusted his supporters and cost him the election.

Lovely thought of the *Globe* article he had read earlier in the week: "Mayor Says No to Governor Race." A state Democratic Party leader had expressed hope that Riordan would change his mind, noting that the deadline for entering the primary was still a month away. David Kantor had said he was going to try to straighten things out with the Chosen Few "after," and that "after" was a month away. Lovely wondered what nasty surprise the Chosen Few had in store for Governor Aldrich.

Fifteen minutes later, Lovely turned onto Roland Moore's street. Moore lived in Weston, a bedroom community half an hour from Boston, in a neighborhood of large contemporary homes on wooded lots. His house was a sprawling, one-story structure made mostly of glass, set back at the end of a fifty-yard driveway. Moore had called Lovely's landline, so Judy would have recorded the call. But she might not have been monitoring the call in real time, and might not know Lovely was on his way. Lovely hoped this was the case. He drove a quarter mile past the house and parked on the side of the road. He wasn't taking any chances this time. If Judy showed up, he would wait behind the door, then cover her with his gun and search her for weapons.

Lovely glanced at his watch. 9:10 p.m. Judy would be arriving in twenty minutes. He locked his car and headed back toward Moore's house at a half-run. He needed time to give Moore his instructions and prepare him for contingencies. Lovely reached Moore's driveway and slowed to a walk. The lawn was glistening with dew. Somewhere in the distance, a dog was barking. It stopped, and Lovely could hear tree frogs trilling in the woods. He walked up the gravel path to the front entrance. Inside, the lights were on and the drapes were closed, making the house appear to glow. Lovely rapped the knocker on the oversized wooden door. It opened. Judy Winter stood in front of him, feet spread wide, pointing a gun at his chest.

CHAPTER THIRTY-FIVE

"Hands behind your head," Judy said. Her expression was one of concentration, like the face of an Olympic diver photographed just before leaving the board.

Lovely's hands went up. Her gun was a Ruger .357 Magnum, identical to the one in his holster except for the silencer attached to the muzzle. She wore a navy blue miniskirt and matching vest. She had a cell phone on her belt.

"Step inside," she said. "Slowly."

She backed away as Lovely went in, then closed the door behind him. Beneath the scent of her perfume, he caught the faint, familiar, chemical smell he had noticed the night before.

"Through that door on your right," she said.

Lovely stepped through the doorway into the living room. Roland Moore was lying on his Isfahan Oriental carpet. There was a bullet hole in the center of his forehead and his face was awash with blood.

Lovely's eyes sagged shut. *Oh, God, Roland.* He should have seen this coming. Moore would have been able to testify to the connection between Andrew Winthrop and the thin man. With Lovely threatening to expose the Chosen Few, the group must have decided Moore had to go.

"Sit in that chair," Judy said.

There were two matching leather chairs facing the couch, separated by a small glass table. Lovely sat in the one nearest him. Judy stood on his right, five feet away.

"Lower your hands slowly and tuck them under your thighs."

Lovely did as he was told. She raised her gun to the level of his temple and came toward him. In a rush, he realized what was happening: Her gun was his own spare. She had seen him stow his Ruger in the closet, so she told the thin man to check the spot for a weapon. Lovely had strapped on his regular gun before he left for Star Market, but the thin man had found his spare. She had shot Moore with Lovely's gun. She would have overheard Lovely's conversations with Jaimee, so she knew there was a budding interest between them. And she had used Lovely's phone, so she had seen the paper, stabbed to his desk with an X-acto knife, which had Moore's name on it and the word "asshole" written across it. She was going to stage the scene to look like a murder-suicide.

To make it believable, Judy would have to bring the gun close enough for the shot to cause powder burns around the entry wound. As a pro, she would know that. Out of the corner of his eye, Lovely watched the muzzle of the Ruger moving straight toward his right temple. His last thought was she had her tongue in my mouth last night, and now she's going to kill me.

Lovely jerked his hand straight up at her wrist and ducked forward. He heard a pop and felt the bullet's compression wave on the back of his head. Glass shattered somewhere in the room. Lovely's nostrils filled with the acrid scent of burnt powder. Still bent over, he made a frantic grab for Judy's gun. His hand latched onto her forearm, just below the elbow. She bent her arm to free it. He had no leverage and could feel his fingers slipping. The muzzle of her gun was moving toward him. He freed his other hand and grabbed the gun by the cylinder. It went off again, burying a slug in the back of his chair. He stood up and wrenched the weapon out of Judy's grip. She kicked him in the groin. He collapsed on the floor, clutching the gun to his chest like a life preserver. He heard her run down the hall and out the front door. Her footsteps made a staccato sound on the driveway. The sound stopped.

Lovely was lying in a fetal position on Moore's Isfahan rug, gasping for breath. He guessed Judy was calling the thin man on her cell phone. He would be waiting nearby. She was going to get away and Lovely couldn't stop her.

170

A minute passed. The pain began to subside. Lovely heard a car screech to a stop out front. He hauled himself to a sitting position. He had to get a look at the car. Outside, a door slammed and an engine roared. Lovely made it to the window in time to see an empty street.

He hobbled over to Moore and pressed his fingers against Moore's throat. No pulse. His skin felt cool. No one could survive a shot in the forehead with a .357 Magnum. Lovely turned away, overwhelmed by a wave of sadness and despair.

He went to the phone and dialed 911. He told the police who he was and what had happened. He gave them a description of Judy and the thin man and related what he knew about their cars. When he finished the call, he noticed he was still clutching his spare Ruger. He reached into his pocket for a handkerchief to wrap around it, so he wouldn't smudge Judy's fingerprints any more than he already had. Her prints would be all over the house, too, and in Lovely's... The thought froze. He had just remembered what the familiar chemical smell was: New Skin, an aerosol plastic available in drug stores for use as a bandage. It could be applied over the fingertips to mask prints. The technique was as effective as wearing gloves, and much less conspicuous. The only prints on the gun would be Lovely's.

Judy would have left no prints in the house, either, or in Lovely's apartment. He had no license plate number for her car, even though it had been parked in front of his porch for half an hour. Her name was undoubtedly fake, as was the thin man's, and Lovely had no address or telephone number for either of them. And here he was, in Moore's house, holding the murder weapon which was registered in his own name, his car stashed on the side of the road a quarter mile away, planning to blame the murder on someone who didn't exist. He was going to have a tough time selling his story to the police. Lovely heard a siren wail in the distance.

His thoughts turned to Judy and the thin man. Their plan must have been to dispatch Moore and Lovely, then drive out to Ashton and take out David Kantor. With Lovely still alive, they couldn't risk that. They would have to hide or run. Were they on their way back to Tremont Street?

Lovely could hear the siren getting closer. If he waited for the cops, they'd detain him for hours, question him, possibly even arrest him. He took a last look at Roland. Then he pocketed the murder weapon and went out the front door. He ran down the street to his Chrysler. As he climbed in, he saw a police car turn into Moore's driveway, lights flashing. Lovely sped off down the road.

CHAPTER THIRTY-SIX

As soon as he was out of sight of Moore's house, Lovely picked up the phone and called Jaimee.

"I don't have time to explain myself," he said. "Just listen. I need you to watch Tremont Street from your window. I'm pretty sure two people, a man and a woman, are going to arrive soon. Write this down." He waited while she found a pen. "They may be in a white Honda Civic or a dark-colored sedan. The man is tall and thin. The woman will be wearing a navy blue miniskirt and vest. They'll go into a building on the other side of Tremont Street, either on your block or the next one down toward Mass Ave. I need to know the building. All right?"

"I'll do my best."

"Thanks. I'll be there in twenty minutes."

Lovely merged onto the Turnpike and sped toward Boston. He reached the outskirts of the city where the highway ran through an industrial zone. The landscape consisted of four lanes of asphalt flanked by railroad tracks and warehouses. Every tree had been cut down long ago, every blade of grass paved over. He passed a speeding passenger train on the parallel tracks. The brightly-lit cars were deserted. Up ahead, the Boston skyline appeared. The Emerald City, he thought. It was like a giant cash machine: you pumped in Harvard lawyers and MBA's, engineers from MIT, and managers from Tufts and BC; you pushed a green button, and out spewed fresh currency. Never mind if a few people got chewed up along the way.

The highway dropped below grade then went underground.

Lovely resurfaced on Huntington Avenue and raced

around the corner to Tremont Street. Jaimee met him at her apartment door.

"I saw a couple go into a building across the street," she said. "I didn't see their car, but the woman was wearing a skirt. The man looked like he might be tall."

"Which building?"

She went to the window. "Third from the end. And the lights in the top floor apartment came on a minute after they went in."

Lovely stared at the brick townhouse in silence. He remembered the pattern of skylights he had noticed the first night on Jaimee's roof, and the head house on the end unit of each block.

"I'm going to take a look into the apartment from the roof," he said.

"Maybe you should call the police."

"If the right people are in there, I will."

Lovely hurried out to his car, grabbed a twelve-inch crowbar from his tool box and crossed the street. He climbed the stone steps in front of the last unit on the block. Through the window of the old oak door, he could see an empty hallway and a carpeted stair winding upward. He put the flat end of the crowbar into the space between the door and the frame, just above the latch, and leaned on the bar. The door was heavy and solidly fastened. He backed up half a step and threw all his weight into the crowbar. The door flew open. Lovely hurried up the stairs to the head house and stepped out on the roof.

The air was cooler than it had been on Jaimee's deck, four nights earlier. That seemed like a long time ago. Down below, the red light was flashing at the intersection. The building Jaimee had pointed out was at the opposite end of the block from the head house, a hundred yards away. Lovely headed across the rooftops at a fast walk. He could hear faint sounds coming from open windows on the front of the townhouses. A television was playing loudly enough for him to make out an over-modulated male voice describing a fatal four-car crash on Route One. A kitchen exhaust fan switched on, pumping a burned odor into the air.

Lovely stopped three buildings from the end and knelt down beside the front skylight. He was looking into the apartment's living room. Two suitcases and a metal trunk were lined up in front of the door. Judy Winter and the thin man were scurrying around, wiping off surfaces with dish rags.

Lovely jumped to his feet. It was too late to call the police—they'd never arrive on time. He glanced back at the head house, a block away. He wasn't even sure he could make it across the roofs, down the stairs, and up the sidewalk to the entrance before Judy and the thin man went out. And he couldn't cover both the front and rear exits. He'd have to stop them now, before they left the apartment.

Lovely glanced at the rear skylight. It was dark. He moved quickly across the roof to the back of the building and peered over the edge. A fire balcony made of iron bars clung to the side of the building, ten feet down. It was barely thirty inches wide, and six feet long from end to end. Forty feet below it, Lovely could see a paved patio furnished with a glass-topped table, wrought-iron chairs, and a charcoal grill. Embers were glowing in the grill.

He stepped back, wiping the sweat off his forehead. Heights had that effect on him. He lay down on his belly, parallel to the edge of the roof, and swung his legs over. He lowered his body until he was hanging from his hands. Dew had dampened the bituminous roof surface and he felt his fingers begin to slip. He glanced down. The movement of his head broke his weakening grip, and he fell.

Lovely landed on the balcony, feet first. He slumped against the building, face against the brick, and sucked in a few lungfulls of air. He pushed away from the wall, shook himself, and moved along the balcony to a window. He was looking into a bedroom. There were no lights on, but the door to the hallway was open, letting in some illumination. He could see a bed beside the window and a mirrored dresser against the far wall. The window was open, leaving only a screen between Lovely and the apartment. He took out his pocket knife and slit the screen from corner to corner. He crawled through onto the bed. It smelled of Judy's perfume. He walked across the carpeted floor to the doorway and drew his Ruger. Judy and the thin man were in the living room, standing by the apartment door. Lovely stepped out into the hall.

"Freeze!" he shouted.

They froze, heads half-turned toward him, open-mouthed. The thin man had short dark hair, bushy eyebrows, and a prominent nose, as Moore had described him. He was wearing a white T-shirt tucked into black denims, and latex gloves. His clothes were too tight to conceal a gun, unless he had something very small in an ankle holster. Judy was still dressed in her skirt and vest. Lovely was almost certain she was unarmed, or she would have shot him after kicking him in the groin at Moore's.

"Put your hands against the wall," Lovely said. "Now spread your legs."

Holding his Ruger in his right hand, Lovely fished his cell phone out of his pocket with his left and glanced at the key pad to dial 911.

In that moment of inattention, the thin man turned and dived on him. He knocked Lovely onto the floor and got a grip on his forearm. Lovely's cell phone went skittering across the floor, but he held on to his Ruger. He wrenched his arm free. Judy ran over and kicked at Lovely's gun hand, catching him on the wrist. The thin man was still on top of him, trying to pin his arms. Judy kicked again. The gun flew out of Lovely's hand. She snatched it up and aimed it at him. He lay still.

"Call Vermino," she said to the thin man. "Quick."

He hurried into the kitchen.

"Mr. Vermino, it's Victor." He spoke with a slight southern accent. "We've got the private eye, Lovely, here in the apartment on Tremont. Yeah, must have followed us from Moore's. What do you want us to do with him? We wiped the place, but there still might be prints, so we can't leave him here, and it would be better not to bloody it up." There was a pause. "Yeah, we're all packed. All we have is our clothes and the equipment we brought up from Georgia." There was another pause. "All right."

Victor came back into the room. Judy was still watching Lovely, covering him with his gun.

"Vermino's on the way," Victor said to her. "He's bringing a vial of Beuthanasia-D and a needle. It's some kind of lethal-injection stuff for dogs. Works on people, too." He nodded toward Lovely. "We'll carry him out the rear door after he's dead and leave him in his car. We can still make it look like a suicide."

Lovely was lying on his back, watching them. While listening to their accents and to Victor's phone conversation, a theory had formed in his mind. These two were from Georgia. Georgia was also the planned location of Governor Aldrich's hunting trip, according to the *Globe* article Lovely had read. The Governor, Lovely guessed, would not come back. He would be shot dead in a "hunting accident," leaving the gubernatorial race wide open for Keith Riordan.

Vermino had hired these two to arrange the assassination. When David Kantor refused to go along with the plan, and threatened to call the police if anything happened to Aldrich, the Chosen Few decided they had to get rid of him. Since Judy and Victor were already involved, Vermino brought them up to Boston to look for David. The old man had made an excellent personnel choice. These two were very businesslike.

Lovely said, "If you kill me, David Kantor will go straight to the police and pin the murder on Vermino and the Chosen Few. He knows what's going on—I told him everything."

"He won't be alive to go the police," Judy said.

Lovely shook his head. "You'll never find him in time. I called him before I left my house and told him to run."

"You were too late."

"Too… What do you mean?"

"Victor was at the Eden Lake Cabins a few hours ago and he put a homing device on David's BMW. We had to take care of you and Moore, first. Soon as we finish here, we'll

177

move on to David. He's going to disappear without a trace. And his wife's going to fall off her balcony."

They were being very thorough. The only person still alive who would know about the Chosen Few would be Adrienne. Maybe her husband figured he could keep her quiet. Even without her, it was a lot of killing. But it wasn't just about winning an election anymore. Now that Lovely had threatened to expose the Chosen Few as criminal conspirators, they were fighting for their lives, and they couldn't afford to leave loose ends.

Lovely had one move left. He still had his spare Ruger, the murder weapon he had taken from Judy, in the side pocket of his jacket.

"Strip the bed," Judy said to Victor. "We can wrap him up in the mattress pad to carry him out."

Judy was still watching Lovely; she had the gun pointed in his direction. Victor was turning to go. Lovely thrust his hand into his pocket. Judy's face contorted with surprise. She leveled the gun at Lovely and squeezed the trigger. For one horrible moment, Lovely's heart seemed to stop beating. Then he pulled out his spare Ruger. The magnetic-ring safety device had worked.

"That gun won't fire," he said to Judy. "But this one will, and right now, I wouldn't think twice about wasting you both."

Lovely moved them back into position against the wall. He knelt down to pick up his cell phone. Just as his hand closed on it, Victor threw himself off the wall and charged. Lovely dropped the phone and fired twice into his chest.

Victor toppled over, his face landing on Lovely's shoe. Lovely turned his gun on Judy. She had followed Victor and was halfway across the room.

"Back on the wall," Lovely said quietly.

She went.

A gurgling noise came from Victor's throat. His leg began to twitch. Lovely stepped backward, freeing his foot, feeling the rush of horror and guilt he always felt when he took a life. Victor's jaw opened and closed convulsively.

Blood spilled out of his mouth onto the carpet. The twitching stopped.

Lovely picked up his cell phone and called the Ant. "I'm in a building on Tremont Street and Vermino's on the way."

The Ant clucked his tongue. "He's the craziest man alive."

"I know. I need you to get over here and wait for him." Lovely gave the Ant the address. "If he sees the police, he'll run, and if he gets away, David Kantor may wind up dead. Didn't you tell me the old man lives at the Four Seasons?"

"Yeah."

"Then he could be here any minute. For all I know, he has keys to this place. I'm up here guarding one of his people, and if he comes in, someone will get killed. Wait for him out front. Just be careful: he's carrying some kind of lethal injection."

"Don't worry."

"Ring the doorbell twice to let me know you're out there."

A minute passed; two; three. Where the hell was the Ant? The Greenhouse was only four blocks away. The doorbell buzzed twice and Lovely let out his breath. A second later, he heard a volley of shots.

Oh, God.

After what seemed like a long time, the door buzzer sounded again. Lovely pushed the intercom button. "Yes?"

"Sorry, Max. I know how you felt about the old guy, but he charged me. I didn't want to get jabbed with that lethal stuff, so I shot him. Like I said, he's the craziest man alive. Or was, anyway."

* * * * *

It was almost midnight when Lovely walked out of the building on Tremont Street. He had spent an hour and a half with the police, giving them his statement and telling them about the Chosen Few. Outside, the night air was cool. A pair of patrol cars stood guard on the street, blue lights flashing.

There was a bloodstain on the sidewalk as big as a manhole cover where Vermino had fallen, shot dead by the Ant's Heckler and Koch nine. Lovely's stomach churned. He turned away.

He glanced up at Jaimee's building. Her lights were off. He had called her soon after the police arrived and told her he would bring her up to date in the morning. The thought of telling her about Moore's death filled him with unimaginable dread. He climbed into his car and drove home.

He had forgotten to feed Cyrus that night, having left in a hurry after the call from Moore, and he expected the cat to be waiting at the door, howling reproachfully. Instead, he found Cyrus asleep on the couch. Lovely walked into his room and stopped short. The top was off the gar's tank.

Lovely switched on the overhead light and bent down in front of the tank. The gar was nowhere in sight. He dropped to his knees, searching the floor. It might have jumped out; it might still be alive. It took Lovely another minute to find it—or what was left of it. The gar's pointed beak lay on the carpet between the aquarium stand and the bed.

Cyrus walked into the room.

"Cyrus," Lovely groaned. "How could you?"

The cat yawned and stretched. He and Lovely stared at each other for a long moment. Then Lovely leaned back against the bed and laughed until his belly ached.

CHAPTER THIRTY-SEVEN

Lovely parked in front of the old church on Columbus Avenue and walked the long block to Tremont Street. He had been awakened that morning by a phone call from David Kantor. Lovely told David what had happened the night before and offered some unsolicited advice. Soon after the call, Lovely left his house, picked up Oz, and drove to Roland Moore's. Lovely had anticipated, correctly, that the police would have left Moore's house locked. Oz picked the lock, and Lovely searched the place until he found what he had come for.

Lovely took a small box out of his car and carried it upstairs to Jaimee's apartment. She was dressed in a short, pale-green bathrobe. Her eyes were red and puffy. Ceci, whose face was also tear-stained, was in her arms. The two-year-old glanced at Lovely, then turned away and buried her face in her mother's shoulder.

"I'm sorry I'm such a mess," Jaimee said. "It's been one of those mornings. David called while I was in the shower and told me about Roland. I was crying, then Ceci started crying."

"Maybe this isn't a good time for us to talk."

"No, it's ok. She's due for a nap anyway."

Ceci turned and looked at him again.

"This is Max," Jaimee said. "He's a friend."

She had her mother's green eyes and long pale lashes. She watched him, becoming interested. She kept her eyes on him for another few seconds then said, "My mommy is sad."

Lovely nodded. "Yes."

She was still watching him.

"That scares you?" he asked.

She nodded glumly.

"Mothers get sad sometimes. She'll be all right."

Ceci looked at Jaimee, who nodded in agreement. The two-year-old didn't seem entirely reassured.

"Nothing you need to do," Lovely said. "She'll stop feeling sad on her own."

This seemed to register, and some of the worry drained from Ceci's face. Jaimee smiled so broadly at Lovely it almost made him blush.

"Have a seat, Max. I'll be right back." She carried Ceci off to bed.

Lovely had never been in the apartment so early in the day. Morning sun was streaming in, lighting up the room. He went to the windows and looked down on Tremont Street. It was Sunday, and not a car was moving. He put down the box he had brought and sat on the couch to wait.

Jaimee returned five minutes later. "Ceci's already asleep." She sat down sideways, facing him.

"I can't tell you how sorry I am about Roland," Lovely said. "He was a good man. I was wrong to suspect him."

Jaimee nodded, blinking back tears. "He was a sweet guy, in spite of everything. He wouldn't have hurt a soul."

"No."

"What happened last night?"

Lovely told her about his encounter with Judy and the thin man.

"You're lucky to be alive," she said grimly.

"Yes."

"What was David's plan? He couldn't have intended to hide out in that cabin forever."

"He figured the Chosen Few wouldn't risk killing Governor Aldrich while he was out there, ready to expose them. He was going to keep out of sight until the Governor returned from his hunting trip and the deadline for entering the primary passed. Then he was going to try to patch things up with them."

"Would he have been able to?"

"I highly doubt it."

"Do you think the plan to kill Aldrich would have

worked if David had gone along with it? I mean, wouldn't the voters have gotten suspicious if Keith had won two come-from-behind elections in such unusual ways?"

"That's why it was so important for the murder to happen now, while Riordan was not in the race. If Aldrich had died in what looked like a hunting accident in a distant state, no one would have dreamed that squeaky-clean Keith Riordan, who wasn't even planning to run for Governor, could have been involved. After Aldrich's death, calls for Riordan to enter the race would have mounted. He probably would have continued refusing for a few more weeks then given in before the deadline to enter the primary. I think the plan would have worked. David saved the Governor's life."

"What will happen to David now?"

"I told him that unless he wants to be a fugitive for the rest of his life, he better consult with a good defense lawyer and tell his story to the police. I think I convinced him."

"You must have—he told me he was going to the police. Will he wind up in jail?"

"I can't imagine he will. He refused to go along with the Aldrich conspiracy. I believe the Chosen Few were behind the scandal that brought down the last mayor. But it's only hearsay, so I didn't mention it to the police. I doubt the story will come out. Even if it does, I'm not sure any laws were broken. I think David will be ok, and I think he learned something from all this. I think Roland's death shook him out of some of his delusions."

"I'd like for something good to have come from all this," Jaimee said. She paused. "Maybe I even learned something. Yesterday, before I knew about Roland's death, I had decided to break things off with him. I realized it just wasn't right for me. So maybe there's a chance for me, yet. Maybe I'll break my addiction to self-destructive men."

"I hope so," Lovely said.

She glanced at him.

"Don't worry, I'm a survivor."

She laughed. "I guess you are, aren't you." Her eyes drifted down to the box at his feet. "What's that?"

"I remembered what you said about the Yanomami Indians drinking the ashes of their dead. So this morning, I went to Roland's house." He opened the box and took out a bottle of wine. The elegant black and gold label bore the words, R.L. Moore, Private Stock. "It's not exactly his ashes, but I thought..."

Jaimee's eyes filled up with tears. She leaned forward and hugged him. Her hair, still damp from the shower, smelled of lavender. Outside, Tremont Street was silent. Sunday's in the South End had a peculiar, sweet stillness. Jaimee released him and leaned back on the sofa. Sunlight from the bay window was shining on her face. Her wet eyes were as green as bottle glass.

"I think something good will come from all this," she said.

"I think so, too."

They drank Roland's ashes and wept.

The End.

About the Author

Matthew Simon grew up in Amherst, Massachusetts and attended Williams College in Williamstown, Massachusetts. He lived and worked in many of Boston's urban neighborhoods, including Back Bay, Beacon Hill, the South End, and Chelsea. Matt spent ten years bedridden with Chronic Fatigue Syndrome. During those years of forced silence, the Max Lovely mystery series evolved as a form of internal entertainment. Matt has since recovered his health.